CARLOS LABBÉ

Translated from
the Spanish by
Will Vanderhyden

NAVIDAD

&

MATANZA

OPEN LETTER
LITERARY TRANSLATIONS FROM THE UNIVERSITY OF ROCHESTER

Copyright © 2007 by Carlos Labbé and Editorial Periférica
Translation copyright © 2014 by Will Vanderhyden

First edition, 2014

Library of Congress Cataloging-in-Publication Data: Available upon request.
ISBN-13: 978-1-934824-92-4 / ISBN-10: 1-934824-92-5

This project is supported in part by an award from
the National Endowment for the Arts.

ART WORKS.
arts.gov

Printed on acid-free paper in the United States of America.

Text set in Dante, a mid-20th-century book typeface designed by Giovanni Mardersteig.
The original type was cut by Charles Malin.

Design by N. J. Furl

Open Letter is the University of Rochester's nonprofit, literary translation press:
Lattimore Hall 411, Box 270082, Rochester, NY 14627

www.openletterbooks.org

NAVIDAD & MATANZA

*To Mónica Ríos and the Labbé Jorqueras.
And to the other six participants of this
novel-game, especially to the ones who
also tried to make it to the final square.*

NAVIDAD
&
MATANZA

I

My name is Domingo. Actually, Domingo is my password here in the laboratory. Just by uttering this name—which I chose—I can enter bedrooms and bathrooms, I can make phone calls, obtain food and drink, access the temperature, hygiene, and communication systems, send and receive email, carry out Internet transactions to purchase any supplies we need. Without it, I'd be trapped in my room. If I were to suffer a psycholinguistic disruption, or if the effect of some microorganism rendered me voiceless, I'd just die of starvation. It's not that my life doesn't matter to anyone; it has to do with the nature of the project. It's not even *top secret*, as we used to joke, rather, to the world, it doesn't exist. So if for some reason I was to forget my name, I wouldn't just die of thirst and hunger, I'd die empirically: the possibility of anyone remembering me would die as well. If the project culminates in success, I'll be able to return to Santiago, get married, have children, maybe make a career as a gastroenterologist. If the project fails, or if I fail, as occurred with Lunes, Miercoles, Jueves, and Viernes—I fear it may be occurring with Sabado—the organization will be sure to eliminate me. You see, my choice of this allegory wasn't made on a whim. The project really does resemble a board game, with dice and squares and all of that. Because there is only one way to stay alive: make it to the end.

2

No TRACE OF ME will remain. For that reason, I've written all of this in code. My password isn't really Domingo. Also, I'll probably insert pieces of pure, hard reality into the story I'm going to tell you. Does that sound okay?

Let this be the beginning: we were seven. Lunes, Martes, Miercoles, Jueves, Viernes, Sabado, and Domingo. We met in 1996, in the Biology Department at Universidad de Chile. We weren't all taking the same classes, but we got acquainted in a creative writing workshop, which was offered as an elective. In a way, our friendship was based in literature. We were the only students in the department interested in what is beyond science. Juan Carlos Montes—you already know that I won't be using real names—is my father. Although that wasn't the only reason he chose us. We were among the best students in the whole School of Sciences. We got the best grades in molecular biology, neuroscience, and genetics. And all of us enjoyed writing stories.

7

ALL OF THIS REMINDS me of the case of Navidad and Matanza, in the summer of 1999. At the time I was writing for a journal whose proprietor was a notorious business executive, and because of this we were tacitly forbidden to write about the most popular topic in the office: disappeared-detainees. This was, of course, during Pinochet's judicial hearing in London. But even more important was the fact that, at the beginning of the year, Judge Guzman had identified the body of our secretary's father in an excavation in the Atacama Desert. Suddenly what had been a really worn out subject took on an archaic and distant force that came to completely disrupt our work environment. And so, I'm not sure if it was out of blind solidarity, or a desire to get out of the office, but during those two months we journalists felt oddly compelled to investigate, anywhere we could, news of abductions, disappearances, or reports of missing persons in the province. I began looking into the case of a brother and sister who disappeared in Navidad.

Navidad, a small town in Region VI, is the gateway to that obscure stretch of coastline between Santo Domingo and Pichilemu. A couple miles farther along is its twin village, the no less bucolic beach town, Matanza. The area enjoyed several months of touristic splendor when the secret VIP club of a famed international resort temporarily occupied the beach during the last summer of the past millennium. There are about ten thousand members in this club who, every five years via unknown channels, receive conceptual instructions and coordinates of latitude and longitude announcing the unfolding of a unique, unprecedented event. That year, the members received at their doors a young Australian man who handed them an invitation and recited a supposedly unpublished poem by Edgar Lee Masters entitled "The Hotel Room," in whose final lines appeared the password: "Transensorial beyond seasons / the Spanish groom said / *matanza y natividad*, heaven and hell."

The business executive Jose Francisco Vivar recalls that his family received the Australian visitor in September of 1998. Vivar knew it was a representative of the VIP club and he was pleased the event was going to take place in Chile. Since the trip to Navidad wouldn't be that expensive, he'd be able to bring along his wife and their two children, Bruno (then 19) and Alicia (14). "I have nothing else to add," he said, in a report in a daily newspaper from that time, "just that after twenty years of enjoying these events of infinite relaxation, alone or with my wife, I thought the experience would be even better with my whole family. But that was not the case." At that point, according to the report, Jose Francisco Vivar broke down. "We'd been in Navidad for two weeks. One afternoon, a Thursday, Teresa and I left the children, who wanted to stay at the beach a while longer. We went back to the hotel where we showered, changed clothes, and got something to eat. At seven we planned to meet the children in the Room of Shadows, a site the organization had set up to put on a variety of shows, a sort of Matanza bazaar. That night, Patrice Dounn, the Congolese thereminist was performing." But Jose Francisco and Teresa never saw their two children again. The image of the two youths shouting goodbye and running toward the waves is the last that they have. Alicia and Bruno officially disappeared the afternoon of January 18th, 1999.

10

To THIS DAY, police investigators have continued to add sightings of Bruno Vivar to the case file of the disappeared Navidad siblings. Every summer since the disappearance, a dozen witnesses from different areas of the central coast have reported seeing a young man fitting his description: striped T-shirt in various combinations of primary colors; shorts or bathing trunks; leather sandals; extremely thin, hairless legs; disheveled, raggedly-cut hair, sometimes brown, sometimes dyed red. As if the last image his parents had of him remained burned on the retinas of so many people who never knew him (the press coverage was as intense as it was brief), they always see Bruno Vivar lying on the sand, face down on his towel, staring out to sea, looking disdainfully through some photographs, or swimming in silence. Of course, other accounts add specific and equally disturbing details: drinking in hotel bars, beer from cans or double shots of whiskey which he pays for with a credit card issued in the United States, while with the other hand he caresses a die which he spins like a top on the lacquered surface of the bar; sitting on a terrace at noon, noisily eating French fries; reading, in the dining hall, a letter delivered to the hotel weeks before; rolling the die and then writing another letter never sent by local mail.

This information comes from diverse sources: guards, waiters, clerks, receptionists, and janitors, who, at the time, also hoped to put together the case's missing pieces, but who only succeeded in helping the police declare unverifiable the possibilities of homicide or kidnapping. It has been tacitly assumed that Bruno Vivar—a legal adult—simply abandoned his family without warning, which is not a crime in Chile.

The most perplexing question is why the name of Alicia Vivar, the fourteen-year-old girl, appears only twice in the case file. Especially after reviewing in detail the reports of repeated sightings of her brother, Bruno. Because Bruno has never once reappeared alone. The accounts agree that he arrives at hotel parking lots in a variety of expensive cars always driven by a man whose smile also appears in police archives, although in another section: Boris Real.

Boris Real became known in Chile in 1984 as the young Chilean executive who, representing a group of Swiss investors wanting to buy Petrohue Bank, ended up in the Capuchinos jail as a result of an antimonopoly suit filed by the Superintendent of Banks, when it was confirmed that the Swiss were linked to an Australian investment group that had acquired the Atacama Bank and, also to a Spanish-Norwegian group that acquired De Los Lagos Bank and Antonio Varas Bank. He was tried as the representative of the inscrutable international consortium that attempted to acquire fifty-one percent of Chilean banks, a move that, it is noted, could have had consequences for our country beyond the strictly financial. The group in question immediately withdrew from the country, leaving no discernible trace. At least until the summer of 1999. Of course, Boris Real was not that man's actual name. It was the alias of Francisco Virditti (41), who admitted to having headed a group of six shareholders motivated by "nothing more than the legitimate game of the market," as he stated in the only interview he's ever given.

Seven years later, when the Chilean press scarcely recalled the business conspiracies that helped prevent analysis of the Pinochet recession, there came the unfortunate death of Juan Ausencio Martínez Salas. February fifth, on the seventeenth hole of the Prince of Wales Golf Club, a heart attack ended the days of the Undersecretary of Education of Patricio Aylwin's administration. That afternoon, Martínez Salas was strolling the links of the capital's golf club in the company of two friends from his time as an MBA student at the University of Chicago: an executive in the board and video game industry Jose Francisco Vivar, and Boris Real. A check of the witnesses in the Civil Register reveals that the given name of the executive who was present at the moment of death is Boris Real Yañez (48), and there is no request for a change of name associated with his identity. Perhaps it was another Boris Real; perhaps Francisco Virditti was the real pseudonym. Nevertheless, another newspaper photograph, which shows Real speaking about his dear friend, reveals the face of the same businessman who declared himself innocent in front of the Superintendent of Banks in 1984. In a press conference on the 16th of May 1995, congressman Nelson Avila denounced the possibility of a secret murder plot when the autopsy results for undersecretary Martínez Salas suggested traces of poison in his system. Public shock lasted two days. As so often happens, there was talk of political crisis, but no particular individual was implicated. Soon everything was forgotten. Boris Real was subpoenaed in his Vitacura residence before returning to anonymity. Various accounts report that he made a statement to Irma Sepulveda, the judge in charge of the trial investigating the death of Martínez Salas. Today it's almost impossible to find Boris

Real; he has no known residence and his name doesn't appear in any public record. Approached by the press in the days following his children's disappearance, Jose Francisco Vivar stated that he was no longer in contact with his friend.

Even more disturbing, one evening in July of 1997, with my own eyes I saw Vivar, Boris Real, and congressman Nelson Avila walking on the beach in Cachagua. They were accompanied by their respective children. Of course I urged my companion to surreptitiously eavesdrop with me. The situation only became relevant for me after I started investigating the incidents in Navidad and Matanza: Boris Real was walking hand in hand with little Alicia Vivar, then a girl of twelve. They were walking a slight distance behind the rest of the group. She asked him to go with her to the rocks to look for seashells. She didn't address him formally or call him uncle, just Boris. Then they talked about the reddish color of the clouds at that time of day and she asked him how long it would be until the end of the world.

14

THAT SUMMER THEY traversed the beaches of Chile's central coast in a Cadillac. Virditti reclined the passenger seat, shut his eyes, and with closed lips, hummed old songs from a tape made for him by a woman years before. "Memories Are Made of This" could be heard. He took drags on a cigar now and then, that being the only movement indicating to someone watching from outside that he wasn't asleep. Specifically for someone watching from the other side of the beach; there I was on my towel, lying down, with a pair of binoculars. Alicia was at my side. Or rather: she occasionally came shivering from the sea to lie down beside me, clutching her arms tightly against the longed-for skin of her body. I dropped my binoculars, picked up a handful of sand, and let it fall delicately along the path traced by the freckles on her back between her shoulder blades down to her waist. But she didn't smile. With closed eyes she murmured, *Fist-fuck*, and only upon hearing this immensely disturbing expression she reminded me that she wasn't happy and never would be. Those nights she spoke to me in English, from her room across the hotel hallway, in a voice hoarse with weeping or laughter, the voice of a woman who has pissed herself laughing. She told me terrible stories of children that transformed into the story of her nightmares: a rabbit walking by, her on top of another woman whom I also love, sucking on her dried-up breast, unaware. On top of a grave. Brazenly she said: The grave into which I'm now staring. Would you like to know what I see?

Obviously, the Alicia of whom I speak is not the same girl of fourteen, at least not the Alicia Vivar for whom the police are still searching. She stood up; she went running toward the sea. She kicked sand in my eyes. For peeking! she shouted. So I ran after her, grabbing her, the waves already over our shoulders, and held her underwater with the weight of my whole body for half a minute. She came up gasping and didn't want to speak to me. Then I took her face in my hands and said to her: My little girl, my lost one, my indecipherable book. Sure, moron, your little girl my ass, she responded and then leaned in and bit my lip. This is what I had to discover. That we'll never be allowed to experience a desire we simply cannot handle. I write this for her, wherever she is. For me, this report will not be neutral: hundreds of connotations have imposed themselves between me and her, because I was naïve enough to think that love has something to do with words, with the proper use of them. Now I'm afraid to speak; I'll just become a professional. But there is one truth. I loved Alicia. Above all: I love her still. Whatever name she has now.

That's the reason I write at this late hour. Returning after forty hours of work in the laboratory. Drunk. Alone. Lost. With my head in the grave. I know what's right, what awaits me, and the splendor. Glimpses. I also know that sometimes in the Cadillac, Francisco Virditti opened his eyes and watched how Bruno headed for the beach wearing nothing but a bathing suit. Virditti knew perfectly well which girl Bruno had chosen that afternoon, all of them different, but resembling each other in the unfathomable. Bruno would get ready to go in the water and dive in next to them, make a disarming joke, laugh, a sidelong glance, and manage to randomly brush up against them in the salt and the spray. And, after ten minutes, the girl, moved by Bruno Vivar's purple lips, would offer to share her towel with him. This was the moment they waited for, when they arrived where her things had been, the girl would pale to find her towels had been stolen. Her face would empty. It reminded me of my sister; or rather, the daughter of my father, Bruno would tell me much later, between two whiskeys, confronting a death threat: one that I made. Arrogant, twisted, motherfucking fool. If I had him in front of me now I wouldn't let him speak. I'd spit on him and kick the shit out of him. There's nothing more to say. At that same moment, in the car, Virditti was dying of laughter. He'd managed to cross the beach, take the towels, and return coolly to the passenger seat of the Cadillac, while Bruno plied his charms amid the waves. But the game was interrupted when Alicia decided to wait for Francisco Virditti in the backseat of the Cadillac and greet him: Fool, you're the one I was looking for. I realize there was nothing I could've done to stop her. Then he started the car and flew toward the highway. Out there, where death so often dwells.

20

I WANT TO TELL you how we imagine the organization's facilities outside the walls of the six bedrooms, the entertainment room, meeting room, bathrooms, and laboratory where they've locked us. Our idea is based on the few things Juan Carlos Montes has told us, and the din we sometimes hear in the night. There's a bubbling machine at the center of a four-hundred-and-sixty square foot industrial plant, beneath a remote mountain, desert, or glacier in the United States. Thick tubes surround it, running through lead walls that contain the radioactive chemicals. In the center there's a glass dome where the intangible, glowing substance we call hadón reacts. Everything painted blue and white. Cold bulbs that do not light or flicker. As in our dormitories, a reflective panel covers the surface of the walls, ceilings, and floor. But it's not a mirror. Everything it reflects forms part of the surveillance record at the Masters Lab. It's also the medium they use to communicate: sometimes in the morning you might be getting dressed, brushing your teeth, or simply examining your face or your back in the mirror, and your image disappears, like a stone thrown into a pool. The reflection reforms, but now it's the face of someone else, in some other location, materializing to tell you something.

And so it was this morning. Immediately my reflection transformed into Montes, informing me that we had a very important matter to discuss that afternoon. I speculated that it had to do with the chapters of the novel-game Martes and I had recently written. Montes would ask us to end this diversion. He wouldn't have been pleased with the story about the girl and the father who swim in the sea while their towels are stolen, because he would have recognized, first the appearances of Edgar Lee Masters and Real (coincidences, he might surmise at first) and then of the hadón and the Vivars, as a rabidly explicit protest on our part against the silencing of Sabado, who'd been locked in her bedroom for more than a month. I feared the worst.

I sat down to wait in one of the meeting room's translucent chairs. As my eyes followed, on the screen of the table's central panel, three-dimensional simulations of genetically amnesic mice passively reacting to hadón (before normal mice, also hadonized, devoured them furiously), I entertained myself by planning the disappearance of the journalist, whom I'd succeeded in establishing as the protagonist-narrator confronting the truth of the Vivar case: there was no truth. It was all a farce. Maybe it'd have something to do with some scheme of Boris Real's to divert suspicion regarding his involvement in the accident at the Vivar's family pool that took the lives of Juan Carlos Montes's two children. Maybe it'd simply be related to thoughts Alicia wrote down in the notebook she hid in horror under her bed every time her father tapped softly at her door, coming in to tell her the same story he told every night, *Alice in the Underworld*; the same notebook that the journalist would find in the glove compartment of his car on his way back to Santiago, the handwriting so similar to his own that it made him doubt his sanity.

I was lost in these musings when the sliding door blinked open and shut. Juan Carlos Montes, pale and scowling, stood in front of me. He explained that the project had come to an end. He wanted me to know that his father was a great scientist. A specialist, respected equally in the logic and metaphysics of quantum theory, as well as in behavioral predictions given limited variables. So, while we were developing a chemical meant to inhibit all social impulses in mice, Montes's father was testing how we— seven human beings subjected to a limited routine, limited spatial and temporal freedom, to emotional relations regulated by light, ambient temperature, and the most awful food and music—would respond to his disintegration hypothesis. So he'd let us play at this idiotic email novel, even though we spoke ill of him, believing access to our inboxes to be personal and private. Everyone's subjectivity would be more compromised in a literary creation than in the work of synthesizing hadón, and it was to their advantage that the course of our aggravation, fear, hate, and inevitable conflict be recorded in the first person. His father was a man of acute perspicacity, he told me. He'd projected a rule of analogous synchrony, predicting that, in the moment Martes, Sabado, and I finally arrived at a form of hadón a human metabolism could tolerate, our relationship would disintegrate, fatally. As an homage to our work, the video of our sojourn in the laboratory would be used by Montes before the OMS commission as proof that, in reality, human beings do not require ad campaigns or drug therapy to feel hate, they possess an instinctive propensity for it. So, the supposed side effects of hadón could only be presumed, never proven.

Nothing that Juan Carlos Montes said surprised me. I listened to him without confusion or hope, like someone reading a book or watching a movie. He told me that now they were going to shut me in a room with Martes until one of us destroyed the other. Whoever was left alive would be allowed to leave with a bank account containing a considerable sum and no memory of the last ten months. Then I asked about Sabado. Montes took a step back and told me that she was no longer in her bedroom, or in any other area of the laboratory. Although it seemed impossible, she'd managed to escape through the air ducts in the bathroom or the entertainment room. It was likely that no one would ever see her again. She'd spend a few days slithering through the underground sewer system of the industrial complex, looking desperately for a way to the surface. But she wouldn't find one. Sabado would die of starvation or gangrene in the *Underworld*, Montes said ironically. I could take no more; I stood up loudly from my chair and jumped on him, spitting. I remember stomping on his head until his face was paler than before. My foot looked like a boot of blood.

I went to the entertainment room and sat down at my computer. I checked my email. There was a laconic but affectionate message from Sabado. She'd sent it in the last five minutes from a coffee house in downtown Salt Lake City. She said she was safe. That she knew that today they'd add doses of hadón, experimentally processed for human beings, to our food. She also attached one of the final episodes of the novel-game, which I'll send to you later.

Martes just came in. He's sweating and looking at me as if he doesn't trust, as if he doesn't trust me, or something around me. I should go. The door just locked from the outside, I fear permanently.

26

MORE THAN JUST A family, it doesn't seem presumptuous to state that the Vivars were a group of people bound together by an enduring perplexity, by having in common something more than possessive impulses. The magazine articles that appeared in the months following Bruno and Alicia's disappearance—the first of which I wrote myself (*Revista SEA*, n° 327, February 24th, 1999)—had nothing to do with reality.

Photographs of the family smiling and embracing each other in the warmth of their home were only part of the media campaign orchestrated by Teresa Elena Virditti. It was no coincidence that, following the disappearance of his two children, Juan Francisco Vivar shut himself away in his mansion. I'm talking about pathological individuals; six twisted people taking part in an unpredictable game.

The article in *SEA*, contrary to what the date of publication indicates, wasn't written in response to the events in Navidad and Matanza, nor did the photograph depicting the Vivars necessarily come from the *Vivar Family Archive*, as the caption states. In the last days of December—less than a month before Bruno and Alicia disappeared—the journal's photographer and I received instructions to "write a human interest piece" on the family of renowned businessman Jose Francisco Vivar. As usual, with a roll of our eyes, we obeyed; in the end our salaries, like all the funds at the journal, came from these people, and they were committed to maintaining an image of homespun happiness. And really it wasn't at all surprising since the fastidious Teresa Elena Virditti (with her unforgettable opera goer hairstyle) was, at the time, on *SEA's* editorial committee. Only after being in that house and hearing the news of the disappearance of those two children—which didn't surprise me—can I explain the shudder I experience when I read that the Chilean family is the moral foundation of our country's ruling class.

The interview was scheduled for a Friday at seven in the evening so the whole family could be there. We arrived—the photographer and I—a little early to their residence in Los Dominicos; we picked it out by the imposing grey wall that surrounded it. We buzzed the intercom and were received and asked to wait by the butler, a man of refined manners whose nose was so small that at first glance he appeared not to have one. This detail is not trivial. Soon the mistress of the house, señora Teresa Elena, whom we'd met previously, arrived. She gave instructions to the butler; she called him Bonito. The first surprise was the nose-less Bonito's response to her instructions; he let out a low laugh, murmuring: I don't believe you, you filthy sow, and off he went, disappearing down the stairs. In that moment, I expected a scene to unfold: the woman firing Bonito, bemoaning the lack of respect, getting all flustered. But nothing happened. The man wasn't just a butler, as I found out later. Señora Terelenita, as her friends called her, was distracted for a moment. Then she shook our hands again and left us alone.

We should've waited, as they requested, in that hallway adorned with oil paintings of English hunting scenes and illustrations of bad golf jokes. But it just so happened that my coworker needed to use the bathroom. His situation was so urgent that, instead of calling the butler for assistance, he decided to go look for it on his own. Meanwhile, I stood looking out at the home's vast estate through the thick glass that served as a wall in the entrance hallway. The house dropped three stories, completely covering the eastern slope of the hill. I noted the care with which the trees had been planted along the other side of the hill to the north, bordering a grassy brown pathway that, from the height where I was standing, I saw intersect another pathway, defined by a variety of grasses in differing shades of green. In the middle of this lushness, I caught sight of two figures. A beautiful young woman, dressed in a bikini, walked out through the trees that concealed the swimming pool. She was short with long hair falling down her back. She held a striped towel in her right hand. In her other hand, she carried another towel (or a robe). It was very white. So white that the reddish, almost black stain on one corner stood out starkly. Every so often she stopped and rubbed her eyes. I thought she was crying. But I was mistaken: later, in the living room, she would repeat this gesture, and her brother, holding her hand, would give her a light slap, saying: Stop it, to which she would respond, yawning: I'm sleepy. And then she would look at me maliciously so that I would stop staring at her. But there, standing in front of that large window, it looked like she was crying. I saw that the stain extended to her body, to her left leg, her left thigh. It must be blood, I thought. Her first period must have come unexpectedly and because of this she was in pain.

The other figure moved through the park from the southeast, along the brown grass pathway. It was difficult to tell who it was. At a glance it looked like a woman, judging by the dress, the jewelry, and the fashionable hairdo. But whoever it was walked in a distinct way, legs wide apart, which made me doubt, correctly, that it was señora Terelenita. Then the figure took off the wig and threw it in the bushes, the dress too, stashing it behind a lavish Georgian dollhouse, another station on that pathway of playthings.

The figure wasn't wearing a bra or panties. He laid down on the grass (it was clearly a man), naked, with a visible erection. It looked like he was carrying some sort of list in one hand. I imagined that it enumerated how many steps away the little girl was. After five steps she still hadn't reached him, no: the garden's sprinklers came on. All at once. The man's naked body was soaked; he closed his eyes and pounded his fists on the grass like an impatient child. His erection shrunk. Soon the girl saw him. She wasn't surprised, nor did she stop, instead she walked over and sat down next to him. The man, dripping wet, sat up and pulled her small body against his. She in a bikini, he naked.

It was hot and the grass was sopping. The scene struck me as sordid, especially witnessed through sheets and sheets of water shooting from sprinklers, like iridescent specters in front of the light. I shut my eyes and turned around. I didn't know what to do: I'm not sure how I reacted, but suddenly I felt someone softly blowing on my eyelids. When I opened my eyes, scandalized, I saw that I was one step away from Bonito, the butler or whatever he was. He placed one hand on my shoulder and, with the other, offered me a glass of Coke. Calm down, he whispered. Alarmed, I stammered and pointed out the window, but he'd already disappeared. I brought the glass to my lips. There was no one outside. The girl's towels had been left in a tangle on the grass and a Great Dane was pushing them with her nose toward an area underneath a birch tree occupied by another dollhouse, this one of Mediterranean style.

Soon my colleague, the photographer, came back, out of breath. He looked anxiously in all directions. You're pale, he said to me. So are you, I replied. It wasn't necessary to ask him anything; immediately he began his confused tale, which he described more than once as "a terrible error." Looking for the bathroom, he'd come across a room where a hairless boy, lying in bed, was observing a large aquarium, which occupied more than half of one wall. According to the photographer, the "terrible error" had nothing to do with his own impertinence, but with what was inside the aquarium. They weren't fish, though, in a way, they seemed to be: three little girls with long hair swam about without needing to come up for air. The three small sirens came together for a moment behind the glass, staring with curiosity at the unfamiliar man who'd just walked in. The photographer ran out into the hallway without being seen by the boy. Their faces, if you could've seen them. They were horrible. Expressionless, like all beings that live underwater, but they were little girls. Monsters, he'd just said when the butler reappeared in a doorway and said that the family was waiting in the living room. Unsettled as we were, we decided to finish the job as quickly as possible. I should add that I was more intrigued than afraid.

The interview lasted forty-five minutes. My companion took half a roll of photographs before excusing himself, saying he felt ill. He left the house and waited for me in the car. The Vivars were arranged on the couch so that a chimney and chandelier were also in the shot. They were a very affectionate family: Juan Francisco Vivar sat with his wife on his lap; Bruno—his head shaved—placed his right arm on his father's back while holding his mother's hand; Alicia rested her head on Bruno's chest and he patted her lightly on the cheek. To my surprise, Bonito stayed, seated on the arm of the couch, twirling the girl's long locks between his fingers. He even spoke occasionally. Discounting the excessive displays of mutual affection that I'd witnessed, the interview answered many of my questions. Juan Francisco Vivar's hair was gelled, his hands well manicured. At one point, I noticed the sheen of moisture behind his ears: sprinkler water from the garden, I suspected. Although clearly Alicia seemed to be in another world (as adolescents generally are, I should add), she didn't seem particularly unhappy. They even laughed together recounting an anecdote about sledding near the hot springs in Chillán. There was a kind of excessive sincerity in that family: it provoked feelings of anxiety. The mistress of the house gave me a strange look, something like a smile, when she walked me to the door, and recited the names of everyone living in the house: besides her children and husband there was the foreign cook and Violeta, the Great Dane. Bonito, pardon, Boris was also staying with them. The man with the strange nose was her brother.

27

(*Revista SEA*, n° 327, February 24th, 1999)

VIVAR VIRDITTI FAMILY: SEQUESTERED HAPPINESS

The kidnapping of Bruno and Alicia, the children of renowned businessman Juan Francisco Vivar and distinguished journalist Teresa Elena Virditti, has shaken the nation. Days before the heartbreaking event, SEA had the opportunity to sit down with the entire happy family.

He greeted us with his characteristic smile and courtesy in the living room of his Los Domincos residence. He stroked the back of his sweet Great Dane Violeta. Four years ago, when Alicia, his little girl, started maturing, Juan Francisco Vivar realized they were going to need a bigger house. "When they were young the kids couldn't sit still. They ran and jumped around all day long, and it dawned on us that what we really needed was a park. The change of scenery has made life more enjoyable. The children have rediscovered nature, and I've always enjoyed golfing, open spaces, horseback riding, and afternoon walks."

Teresa Elena Virditti sat on the couch listening attentively to her husband. Earlier she had shown us the studio and library where she does her work for the journal without neglecting the needs of the family. "For Juan Francisco, the park is the most important thing, but for me there is nothing like my desk," she comments with a smile. That's how the Vivar Virditti's are: an active family. "They were restless when they came out of me," jokes the owner of the board and video game company. Bruno, the eldest son, who is very close to his mother, wanted to major in journalism, but discovered that it was not for him. Now he has taken an interest in biology. "Since I was very young, my father has brought home chemistry sets for my entertainment," he says. Alicia, her parents say, "will be able to do whatever she wants because everything makes her happy." The little girl nods her head and pets the dog. "In this family, everyone has their own space," says Juan Francisco Vivar.

SEA: It must have been fun for your children to grow up surrounded by all the games your company produces.
Juan Francisco Vivar: In truth, yes. At one point I realized that the best way to test a product was to try it out at home. If Bruno and Alicia liked it, the game would be a success among the children of

the nation. Although each one was tested in its own way (Vivar and his daughter laugh). Bruno, for example, performed strength tests on the materials. I'll never forget when I brought home the first videogame, already quite some time ago. And he, accustomed to me bringing him stilts and skateboards, jumped on top of the machine (more laughter from the girl), hoping it would carry him away or something like that. Honestly I think my children are a great indicator of the tastes of Chilean children. They're as healthy and sharp as anyone, I'm glad they're like this. They're happy, they want for nothing, especially affection.

SEA: Your garden demonstrates that you are a family that enjoys outdoor activities.
JFV: Yes, it's odd, but at the same time it makes sense; I've filled the house with board games, but they'd rather go outside.

Teresa Elena Virditti: We have a great love for trees and all things green. My mother planted that oak when she was just a girl. This was part of my great-grandparents estate. The park wasn't so well maintained then; it was a fairly dry garden with lots of wild grass, *de rulo*, as they say in the country. I remember clearly that there was a small forest, and there are still a few of those birch trees left. My sisters and I played hide and seek in that forest and pretended we were camping. I've always said that the children enjoy nature because on my side of the family there have been many great naturalists and botanists.

JFV: And from my side they get their manners, then. (Everyone laughs happily.) In any case, as a family, we're characterized by our taste for fine things. This includes board games, which are proof of the beauty of human ingenuity, of the human mind, which is a marvel, which we also see in video games. It's the same with nature. Every now and then, my wife, Terelenita, and I, we long for some landscape or climate we've not seen for some time. So we travel. For example, at the end of last year we were watching an American Christmas movie, as a family, everyone together in the projection room, when suddenly we were struck by a powerful nostalgia for snow. It'd been several months since we'd experienced that cold, white, exquisite substance; we missed that feeling of enormity. Except for Bruno, who is a skiing fanatic—when there isn't any snow in Santiago he'll go spend a weekend in Europe or Colorado. (Bruno nods, closing his eyes.) He took second place in the '91 season. So, we all went to Switzerland. Why not? We said. We went for a few days. We still laugh recalling when Bruno tried to teach Alicia how ride a sled. He tried to show her how under a pinc tree because it was starting to snow. It was really funny. All of a sudden they realized that the sled had disappeared. They thought someone had taken it without them noticing, but no. The sled went down the hill on its own! Even I was worried when I saw the empty sled show up at the chalet. Tell me that isn't funny. (They all burst out laughing.)

SEA: *So you must already have a trip planned for this summer.*
JFV: The children want to go to the beach. They love swimming in the sea, they look like fish, it's really quite a sight. Yes, we just want to get in the car, head to someplace nearby where the sea is calm, and get in the water. I love swimming in the sea, when I was very young I even swam competitively, at university level.

Besides, both Terelenita and Alicia enjoy the sun, they like to tan. That's why they're so beautiful. But the point is to be together. It'd be nice to take a little trip inside the country and find somewhere to relax. Our beaches are just as beautiful as the great Caribbean or Mediterranean resorts. You have to appreciate what you have, that's why we've already planned to go together as a family—like always—and enjoy the summer here on the central coast. We like to travel, to move, but the most important thing is to be together and to be grateful for the beautiful family we've created.

32

HOSTERIA VERGANZA is located on Highway 5 South, at the exit for the city of San Fernando. It's the closest thing to a hotel you can find between Rancagua and Talca, and so it caught the attention of Boris Real—a lover of comfort, after all—who interrupted his trip to Navidad to stay there on the night of January 12th, 1999. None of the employees remember him, except for Alvaro, the bartender who sometimes plays the piano, because on that night he had to prepare nine double-shots of whiskey and twenty-nine grenadines for the end table where Boris Real and another man, a blonde American or European, sat until sunrise. They conversed quietly, they seemed relaxed, says Alvaro. Every time one of them emptied a glass, they burst out laughing and signaled me, snapping their fingers. The rest of the time they wore impassive expressions. Around sunrise, it seemed to me, they spent two hours staring at each other without blinking. But when the morning light began coming in through the windows, I saw that they each were holding a butter knife in their right hand, and, taking turns, delicately tapping out a tune on wine glasses. At first the sounds were almost imperceptible, but after a few minutes I began to hear sharp, deep, undulating scales. When they were producing a clear melody, one of them half closed his eyes. Seeing this, the other nodded and stopped playing. It seemed like a game, like something invented by children who discover that the piano in the hallway actually works. But this conflicted with their appearance, their impeccable dark suits, their white shirts, their ties, their gelled hair. Around seven-thirty, without a word, they got up from the table. Taking the napkins from their laps, they brushed some crumbs off their jackets. They left some five-dollar bills on the table. The blond man bent over and picked up a heavy, black wooden case that was sitting next to his chair and handed it to the other man. They shook hands. Then they walked down separate hallways to their rooms. Two hours later the blonde man left. The other man left after breakfast, in a Corvette or a Porsche, a car that made an impression on the parking lot attendants.

I reviewed the hotel's register for January of 1999. As I expected, the man to whom some sources attribute the kidnapping of the Vivar siblings wasn't listed. At least not as Boris Real or Francisco Virditti. I asked about the foreigner who'd shared his table the evening of January 12th. Alvaro, the bartender, pointed at the name of Edgar Lee, a Mormon pastor who—visiting Region Six—spent two nights at the Verganza, accompanied by a woman who spent half the day bathing her small child. The housekeeping staff hadn't forgotten them either—the couple had asked to have the sheets changed fourteen times; it was also speculated that they'd stolen some hand towels from the bathroom. Two lines below, on the same page of the register, appears the name of another foreigner: Patrice Dounn. The famous master of the theremin—an unusual instrument whose operation relies on magnetism—who, days later, would perform at the VIP resort in Navidad and Matanza, on the same night that Bruno and Alicia Vivar disappeared. The employees of the Verganza do not remember a dark-skinned guest from that time, despite the fact that the Congolese Dounn is definitely black, as a photograph from n° 695 of *World Music Express* proves. A different page in that same magazine has an article on the theremin: appearing there is a photograph of the black, wooden case, heavy and rectangular, which musicians often use to transport the instrument. It is, without a doubt, the same case that appeared in Alvaro's story; the same case that, in the vicinity of San Fernando, the Mormon pastor Edgar Lee—the American poet, dead in 1950—gave to Patrice Dounn, the Congolese thereminist who, on that exact date, was participating in the performance of *Symphony No. 4 for orchestra (and optional chorus, theremin et alia)*, by Charles Ives, in London's Royal Albert Hall. This would've been an extravagant way to move ten million dollars of hadón, an illegal substance better known as "the ecstasy of hate," upon whose discovery the International Police (Interpol) justified shutting down the festival in Matanza and Navidad on the 19th of January 1999.

34

A FEW DAYS BEFORE the publication of my article in *SEA*, I got a phone call at the journal's office from a one Juan Carlos Montes. I hadn't thought again about the Vivar family, but during that phone conversation I felt, what I'd call now, my first suspicion of the mess the kidnapping of the siblings would uncover. And a certainty: I too would get dirty. Or that I was dirty already. For his part, Montes had no problem beginning the conversation with a lie.

– I live down the street from the Vivar's home. I saw a car with your journal's logo on the door and hoped that finally a journalist with a sense of smell had arrived.

In reality, as I verified later, Juan Carlos Montes not only lived on a different street than he claimed, he lived in a different country.

– Sense of smell?

– I'm calling to find out what sort of story you're writing. If it's not too much trouble, of course.

– Forgive me, but I don't know what you mean by sense of smell.

– A nose.

– Obviously. I don't understand why you're calling.

– Do you like your job at *SEA*?

– Sir, if this is regarding a story you should speak to the editor. It doesn't seem like . . .

– Listen to me. My son was a classmate of Bruno's, the oldest child of the Vivar's. One day Terelenita called us to invite him to a birthday party. I don't know, I guess he was turning five.

– Don't make me hang up. I'm not interested.

I lied.

– At seven in the evening I went across the street to pick up Juan Carlitos. As always, the front door was open and no one greeted me. No doubt Juan Francisco and Terelenita were in their room, you know what I mean.

– No. And I don't see the reason for this conversation. I must insist.

– Please, don't interrupt me, I don't have much time. As I was saying, I went to see if there was anyone in the living room, but the house was empty. A lot of noise was coming from the garden, where the kids were running around and swimming in the pool, watched over by men who looked like house staff. Then all of a sudden I looked at the chimney. It was a reflex. Or I was somehow compelled. I'd seen something that caught my attention, a piece of skin among the flowers. It was hanging from the chimney, it was summer. The piece of skin was . . .

– What?

– A nose. They'd torn off someone's nose and left it stuck to the chimney.

I was silent.

– I don't know if you know who I am. I'm a surgeon, although I don't practice my specialty. I knew right away that it'd been torn off recently. It was still warm.

– A nose?

– Yes. Do you understand now that this little journal where you work doesn't provide you with what you need to write good stories?

– Hang on.

My secretary needed something; I dealt with it as quickly as possible. I picked up the phone:

– Mr. Montes, I'd like to meet with you to discuss this at greater length.

– Yes, yes. But, please, let me finish. I tore a page from a notebook that was in a wastebasket and wrapped the nose inside it.

I was about to put it in my pocket when I heard the children screaming.

– What happened to the nose?

– I left it there, in the living room. I think a big dog came and started chewing on it, something I seem to have seen as I ran as fast I could out to the garden because my son Juan Carlitos had a cramp and was drowning. That's what an employee told me, a butler who worked in the house. I wanted to see my son, but ten large men dressed in suits surrounded the pool. The children were running around wildly, screaming: "The fish, the fish." They were terrified, as if they'd seen a monster. It was horrible. There was a lot of fear and violence and hate, I don't know if I can explain it, a lot of fear and hate in that house.

– Okay. And what happened to your son?

– Juan Carlitos? I couldn't see anything because those guards— who said they were butlers too, but who were speaking into walkie-talkies the whole time—surrounded my son and carried him to a car. They said they were taking him to a clinic, but they didn't say which one. I never saw any of them again. Those fucking criminals evaporated. That was fifteen years ago and I've never seen him since. That's why I'm calling you.

– They took your son?

– They told me he died. Vivar swears my son was never in his house, and he hasn't allowed me to speak to that woman, Terelenita. I filed a report and the police briefly opened an investigation. Shortly thereafter they told me he was dead. The judge said his body might be found in mass grave of disappeared-detainees in Pisagua, but that was another lie. I've spoken with many people and found nothing: my case will never be on television or in the newspapers. I don't want them to discuss the state my wife is in. It pains me even to speak of it.

– Mr. Montes, may I call you later to set up an interview? This is serious. What's your phone number?

– Uh, no, not now. I just want attention put on the Vivar's. I'll call you. Goodbye.

Juan Carlos Montes hung up. I never heard from him again. The old woman who answered the phone at the number from which the call had been made swore at me every time I told her who I was. After what happened in Navidad and Matanza I thought there was an obvious link between the disappearance of the Vivar siblings and Juan Carlitos Montes. But I was wrong. One night in April of 1999, after eating dinner with a friend, I told him about the bizarre story I was interested in writing. My friend, a salesman for a pharmaceutical company, was surprised when I mentioned Juan Carlos Montes.

– Montes? I know Juan Carlos Montes. He hasn't disappeared. He won't leave me alone. He's the product manager of Masters Lab in Chile.

According to my friend, this individual's father, Juan Carlos Montes senior, lived in California; he owned the business.

– A man of means; there's a reason you can't track him down.

Of course, the game's pieces didn't fit together. If this were the same Juan Carlos Montes who'd been kidnapped, according to the story of the man on the telephone, he'd be nineteen years old now. Maybe he was a whiz kid. A boy genius, I said. No, my friend responded, with a smile that reflected the words the man from the telephone had repeated. Hate, fear.

– You have to understand the side effects of hadón, the extremely addicting and popular drug: rapid aging and then death.

I asked him if there was a cure for this addiction. My friend raised his wine glass and made a toast:

– There is nothing that frees us from death, but yes, there is something that frees us from its side effects.

I looked at him, waiting.

– Only perfect love dispels all fear, he quoted.

39

From: Lunes

To: Domingo

Date:

Subject: I heard Alicia singing softly in the elevator, I slipped out and disappeared silently down the stairway, like a disease I felt and continue to feel. The virus of language, the constant use of the illative connotes an obsession.

As always, she'll remove her keys from her backpack full of books, put the key in the lock, enter. But the dark apartment will be filled with a damp, heavy odor that'll make her think of death by drowning, about the water that might exist after such a death, at least about the water that existed before.

I made the horrible sacrifice of ascending in that frightening elevator, and it was all in vain! At any rate, I ran into a cousin of mine in the hallway, such is life. I'm not even sure if this is the right apartment.

XOXO

Lunes

•

From: Martes

To: Domingo

CC: Lunes

Date:

Subject: I might kill her. Better yet: she might never die.

I THINK I HAVE DISAGREEMENTS WITH THE DIRECTION
THE NOVEL IS GOING.

Before sending you my chapter (I've arrived in the silver room
to write my chapter and I notice a disastrous absence: I left the
sheet the board is printed on in my dorm), I wanted to send you
my observations about the novel-game. It seems necessary to better
define the connections, the movement the connections engender,
and the trajectory of the characters. Causes-connections-charac-
ters. To me it seems useful to compare the mass of connections to
a tree. The coherence of each bifurcation (ramification-connection)
is stable at the outset, when they are branches. But as the growing
tree branches out and bifurcates, in addition to specifying the con-
tent of each point, the branches begin to intermingle and cross over
each other. But this only works when the origin of each branch is
well defined. In this way, you can better sketch out the direction
of a novel, with characters and stories, without having a surprising connection distort the narration. This makes the movement
of the story easier to follow for the reader, and narrows down the
millions of interrelations that appear when looking at a mass of,
on their own, flat connections. Another point that seemed a little
bit dicey to me was the inclusion of religious citations. Domingo,

if you want to include particular beliefs in this sort of work, I think it's necessary to clearly define their purpose, especially when it is a purely religious message. When divulging a message, until that message is clear, it suffers; better not to offer mere glimpses that in the end serve no narrative function (really they're just a distraction because they have no contextual significance).

I'm very pleased with what I've read and for that reason and that reason alone I've taken the liberty of criticizing the points that don't live up to my expectations. Which says a lot, because in general my expectations for some people are very high. Well, Domingo, I hope this doesn't seem boring or disappointing, that's all. Chao.

·

FROM: Miercoles
To: Lunes, Martes, Jueves, Viernes, Sabado, Domingo
DATE:
SUBJECT: She'll open the curtains and before she sees how the sun dips below the horizon, even before she sees how her hand ceases to be a hand, passing behind the window's glass to touch it from outside, perplexed, she'll see hundreds of hanging towels. She must've seen the bathtub early in the morning, when, for no reason, she'd gotten up to go look at herself in the bathroom mirror and to see B above her, below her, leading her toward the dunes, in spite of her odor. She must've looked at the bathtub and noticed that I'd left dozens of towels soaking in water of an unpleasant color and aroma. She believes this heap of cloth (can you wring out something that is still underwater?) to be an image from a dream, disappeared in the deepest sleep. So she'll think these towels,

35

stamped with the faces of her friends from the game, pinned to the wall and oozing onto the wallpaper that I chose, are part of a nocturnal terror that will inevitably dissipate when she thinks: No, it's not death, it's life, I'm awake, dry, soft, he's at my side snoring, if I tell him I had a dream, he'll open one eye, embrace me weakly and say: Tell me what you dreamed.

You know? It makes no difference that the rest consider me your invention. The joke doesn't work because two of them know me. Or is it three? Or four? Do you remember? You drank too much whiskey that night in Domingo and Lunes' room. Everyone was there but Sabado, Sabado wasn't invited. Remember? I remember because I was there, more than ever I was there. We played a board game, something involving throwing dice and pondering possible lives, imagining and giving those lives coherence. I don't remember very well, I wasn't paying attention because I dedicated myself to spilling whiskey on the floor of that stupid dormitory, and to stepping in the puddle so that everything got filthy. You remember. Look yourself in the eyes. Don't act like someone who has no memories or emotions. Remember the funny and stupid face Domingo made when he asked you to clean the floor, the stain, and you ignored him. But I looked him silently in the face, mocking myself at the same time, then everyone realized that I was sleeping with you. I don't care if they think I'm quiet just because I don't prattle on like they do. I occupy myself with what's important, you dedicate yourself to the other, to pleasing.

•

Subject: I'll set everything up. Days and hours at her side, talking about love and imitating precisely the behavior and character of her father—dominant, sophisticated, and manipulative, but also attentive, well-meaning, and sometimes a little bit awkward—so she'll want to take care of me as she would him. I won't try to hurt her, on the contrary, I'll try to protect her. Breaking down the memory of the old man, roaming the highway without apparent motive (as far as she can tell), B's Porsche pulling over on the shoulder, B who is sitting in the back seat of the convertible, gesturing and speaking to the old man: Excuse me, can you tell me how to get to the Mormon golf course? And she: a girl wrapped in a towel, chasing B, who at the same time, was chasing a towel wrapped around the small body of a girl. Days and hours acting like the old man, putting my hand on her shoulder so we walk at the same speed, buying her books that she almost likes, almost. Asking her if she enjoyed the movie she went to see with a friend. In short, loving her. Wrapped in towels, of course. And wet. Floating.

When and where is the meeting? I agree that we should create a system that avoids repetition of squares. I also think that if we had more time to develop the fragments the quality would be higher (I've never understood more time as necessarily resulting in longer texts).

Clearly we shouldn't write for children, rather we should write like children (although this might frighten young readers), since it's true that young readers are essentially indefinable (tending to shy away from fixed categories). There's nothing worse than a children's book written for mothers.

With respect to children's books as objects, I think that, as a religious person, you might be interested in something I came across in my research. I don't know if you know this, but one of the first publications exclusively for children was a hieroglyphic bible, that is, text and drawings laid out next to each other, so that a child could read it by describing the drawings (like comics in newspapers). The book is from like the seventeenth century and the pictures of it on the Internet are very odd. It's called *The Hieroglyphical Bible,* you should check it out. I own a book by Lewis Carroll with a prologue by Leopoldo María Panero where he discusses at length why Lewis Carroll wrote for children. The text, written in a slightly schizoid way, is good, and since this theme interests you, I can lend it to you if you'd like.

Well, the words have run out, it remains only for me to give thanks.

•

FROM: Viernes
TO: Lunes, Miercoles, Sabado, Domingo
DATE:
SUBJECT: I'll want you like this: recalling what's forgotten, your face poking out of a dirty pile of sodden towels, panting, sometimes pretty, sometimes ugly, and the saddest thing is that my cruel examination will last only a fraction of a second, because I'll walk by on the avenue and in that moment look absentmindedly up at the window, seeing you covered with dozens of towels like

a zombie. It won't be an insult, just the opposite, the line of the horizon flashing in your pupil, hollow because you're only here, I repeat, for a fraction of a second. I won't be there but I'll see you. Wretched. Remnant. Mine.

Cheers, it's very important that we set up a meeting for the end of the week. We should decide what to do if people land on the same space.

Also we should roll all of the dice. The novel will be bullshit if we only have one day to write; I insist that our texts have a respectable period for development.

I am sending this message to you because I don't know how the hell to send it to everyone at once, I need you to do that for me, thanks.

V.

•

FROM: Sabado

TO: Domingo

DATE:

SUBJECT: She'll enter the room and, as a blast of moisture hits her face, realize that it's been locked all day. She's been out in the street for a long time looking for B. She doesn't know his face, or his name, just the initial. Still, not knowing why, she feels she'll find him. The delicate shape of his head from behind, his shoulders, the name, the quiet, understanding smile, the difficulty speaking, the gelled and messy hair. He might turn around and suggest that they sit down, that they speak, that they search. A passing gleam in which name, face, moisture, laughter, three bears and a wound, a garden, a white stone among many, never alone, please, that gleam that lasts only a fraction of a second and as it appears someone else shares; everything will overlap, no, another word, it'll come together, it'll converge in the name. Soon, however, it'll be of little importance, because curiously, as Rimbaud and the Evangelist simultaneously say, "life is elsewhere." She'll patiently retrieve the towels from the walls, she'll hang them on the balcony, she'll tell him on the phone how strange the prank was, again she'll look for him until he comes.

What do I know? In any case, the fundamental thing is this: we're not fucking infallible, being a Christian is not to be less wrong, or being wrong is not to be bad, or being imperfect is also compatible with success. Maybe you'll meet someone who loves this fragility, the twisting, everything, someone who can also be this way, and everything will be fine. What I told you the other day makes sense, but it doesn't have to be the truth.

Domingo, it's very late. I've already written my brand new episode. Viernes has made you his secretary? I'll do the same, please forward my chapter to everyone. We need to have a meeting, but this weekend I'm leaving and have to leave. I'd like to be at the fucking meeting. Would it be possible to have it sooner? I agree about the repeated squares, but only to a certain extent (it's also fun to watch people organize things to make something new, in one way or another, that isn't identical and fits in every way, variations on a theme, I don't know, for some reason the stories sometimes cross each other but are in a way independent, right? Don't you think?). The timing is a little problematic; it seems the trick would be to write something about the progression. I don't know. Take care.

Sabado

•

From: Domingo

To:

Date: 09/14/2002

Subject: Wet towel. I remember it wrapped around you.

All I do is think about what someone said to me, about what I say, about what I'm saying, about what I'll someday dare to say. I go to my room and write, I come to the silver room and write to you, later I lie down and pray. What I always want is to pray without words, but I'm nowhere near the "full-time mystics." It's just that sometimes words exhaust me. They are, how to put it, communication, tool, pleasure, and doubt. Forgive the complaints and the affectation. I can't avoid it. That is to say, yes I can, but I must speak.

The meeting for the novel-game was brief and insignificant, but now I'll go to bed feeling that everyone had more than enough to say to each other. At least everyone seemed to be happy about having to read and write. Your fragment was praised in passing, by Viernes if I'm not mistaken, as a marvel of concision. Or was it Jueves. I don't know. My words, I stain everything, almost everything, you know. About Wednesday, an open day, regrettably, Viernes suggested that a friend of his write. He says that he has a rational, essayistic style that no one else has. We all agreed. It's worth a shot.

I don't have a strong opinion about the problems you brought up in your email. To my taste everything is fine as we set it up, and I like the idea of people landing on the same square. Forced intertexuality. Goodbye and thank you.

Domingo

45

I MUST ADMIT THAT I abhor articles that begin this way: Life imitates art. I deplore equally both pretentious and self-referential journalism, and above all, journalism that lacks documentation. Art—I am not saying anything particularly original—doesn't imitate life, nor vice versa, for the same reason that people normally hang mirrors in the bathroom or behind the door and not on the bedroom wall facing the bed. This circumlocution serves to justify me: as I listened to Carmen Riza, Alicia Vivar's first grade teacher, an image of myself in this particular moment that I had eight years ago came into my mind. The certainty—though that sounds emphatic—that I'd spend a great deal of time in front of the computer writing an article about an international child-trafficking network. *Narrative anticipation*, a term I'd not heard since my days in university.

When she disappeared, Alicia Vivar was going into eighth grade at Santiago College, where she'd been enrolled since she was four years old. The teacher, Carmen Riza, taught her to read and write, to add and subtract, to know the differences between the kingdoms of the natural world, and also to cut paper with scissors. But mostly she remembered Alicia's exceptional work in violin class.

For more than three years, Alicia composed the variations that a group of fifteen young violinists, accompanied by the teacher on piano, performed during the school's award ceremonies each December. According to Carmen Riza, her Song of the Sand is still played in a civic performance at the end of the year. She didn't excel as a violinist—says Riza—in fact she was the third chair of the second row. But I appreciated her solemnity and that she never placed importance on her ability to invent melodies. She didn't even talk about it. On any given day she'd come in with her lined staves and hand them to me: This is the Song of the Sun, she'd say, this is the Song of the Bush, of the Mean Bear, the Song of Hands, the Song of Evening, those are the ones I remember. It must've been about twenty songs. The only one we didn't perform was the Song of the Corridor. She gave me the sheet and started to cry. She wouldn't tell me what was wrong. Before I sent her home she said quietly: it's just so hard to play.

Alicia Vivar left music behind. When she was ten years old she stopped attending violin class. Instead, according to her classmates, she became interested in rhythmic gymnastics and field hockey. On the topic, Carmen Riza claims to not understand the change, because "the girl had a special ear. It was a loss for the class." But what could Alicia Vivar's musical activities have to do with her disappearance? That is something I can only illustrate with a personal anecdote.

Eight years ago, for no particular reason, I attended a performance by the Santiago College violin class. I went in and sat down without knowing why. It was a Friday afternoon in mid June; it was very cold and the days were passing quickly. I'd recently gotten my degree in journalism and I was looking for a job. Many other things had, regrettably, become much less important. One of those things was fun, just fun, in the abstract, without adjectives or adverbs. What I'd call now, from a certain distance, pleasure. I enjoyed writing stories, novels, poetry, letters to women, Greek comedies, scripts for documentaries. I also enjoyed talking about my writing and the writing of others. To that end, five friends of similar interests and I had come up with a system that, in the beginning, seemed like an original and fascinating discovery. A novel-game. In short, it involved rolling dice, moving your token to a space with prefigured plotlines and formal constraints, writing a text according to those constraints and, that night, mailing this text to the other participants. Everyone had been assigned a day of the week, except Sunday, a day of rest. It was a game of complex rules and seduction. And the result was out of control. However, weeks passed and participants started deserting, for various reasons that were occulted by shame, that "crossroads of love and fear," in the words of a little-known French philosopher we were reading at the time. Already three of my friends—those assigned Monday, Wednesday, and Friday—had stopped participating in the novel-game. A fourth had announced an upcoming trip to New York. We had to decide what was going to happen to the project in light of these desertions.

We decided to meet that Friday, at four in the afternoon, at the Youth and Children's Book Fair, which in those days was held at the Parque Bustamante, in Providencia.

I got there half an hour early. The place was overflowing with red and blue balloons. There were clowns, and people dressed as characters from fairytales, and techno music. I passed by the various editorial stands. At the Pehuen stand, for five hundred pesos,

I bought an anthology of contemporary Canadian poets, which interested me because of the inclusion of Margaret Atwood, one of my favorite novelists at that time. I looked at my watch: it was already four fifteen and no one else had arrived. Then over the loudspeaker they announced that in five minutes the Santiago College violin class would be performing in the amphitheater. I walked toward the venue, deciding to pass the time in one of the plastic chairs. To my left, two mothers were taking pictures; to my right, a little brown-haired girl whose feet didn't reach the floor was applauding soundlessly. On the stage there were three rows of young violinists. Behind them, sat more than fifteen prepubescent girls, whispering, their cheeks burning with embarrassment; they were part of the choir that would accompany the violinists on their last song.

The audience was almost entirely made up of children from different schools, carefree, eating cotton candy. There were some teachers, parents and other relatives who were filming and photographing the musicians. Except for me, lifting my head every five minutes to look around for one of my friends, the only person out of place was a very elegantly dressed man. He stood for the entire performance, arms crossed, wearing dark sunglasses, and a smile that appeared every time the third girl in the second row frowned or glanced at him. I don't remember much about her; she wasn't striking. She was just another girl among those strange, six-year-olds: hair pulled back in a ponytail, thin hands vibrating with the bow, cold face angled over the wood surface of the little violin. The teacher shouted instructions that only the children could hear. F, up down, bow to the audience, next, remember Caro, you begin, louder Alicia. The last song was announced: This is the Song of

Sand, thank you. One three-year-old girl, dressed ridiculously in green, took two steps forward, looked with disturbing seriousness at the teacher, placed the violin under her chin. She waited for two chords from Carmen Riza's electric piano before she began to move her bow. A clean sharp sound lead into a scale, across which the entire section of children's violins joined together in something that sounded to me like Schubert, but sadder, and sicker. Like a child who imagines the music of Schubert after he has learned about Schubert's biography. That's how I felt. I don't know if they were already there, but all of a sudden I noticed that the floor of the stage was covered with pink balloons. In the final crescendo, when the choirgirls stood up and sang, a string on the violin of the little girl alone in the front row broke. Applause erupted. In that moment, without taking the violin from her shoulder, the girl in the second row—who I know now was Alicia Vivar—was the only performer who didn't bow. All alone, she lifted her foot and kicked one of the balloons off the stage, right at the man dressed in the elegant suit, who uncrossed his arms to catch the balloon. I stood, looking at the stage. And in the confusion of congratulating mothers, crying children, and people running from one side to the other, I watched as the girl walked calmly down the steps, went up to the man, and took his hand. He bent down and kissed her cheek. The man was around thirty years old, my age now, I realize. Watching them, I knew where I'd be eight years later, what story I'd be writing right now at my computer. His name was Boris Real. I'm certain that Alicia never composed a single song for the violin. The scores Alicia gave to her teacher were written by Boris Real so that she could perform them. Gifts, you might say. That afternoon they left the Youth and Children's Book Fair holding hands. I felt dirty for what I thought in that moment, and I feel dirty for thinking it now: twenty-four years separated the two of them.

49

WE STOPPED THE CAR at a service station along the highway. We got out to buy a big bottle of ginger ale and took the opportunity to call home. When mother answered we were silent until she started to cry. Then we cried too, and she listened. She always listens though she knows we'll say nothing. Sometimes she laughs, out of pleasure we imagine, because she feels less alone. Then we hang up. It's been twenty-nine years; we'd love to see her. But not father.

We paid the service station attendant to wash the windshield with that tool that collects everything but the last bit of foam. As his face appeared in a corner of the glass, he looked shamelessly inside, and we asked each other if we should make faces at him or direct our gaze toward the infinite. Later we rewrote my last poem, we added an attention grabber, "you remember," which we didn't know if we'd keep. We always do that, add something or remove something when we're bored. Or we read a strange novel aloud, with a flashlight, as we drive through the night. And later we discuss over and over what it was all about.

This was the poem:

DOLLHOUSE

When I'm not looking he comes toward me, when I'm look-ing he stays over there, at a distance, watching me. If I could carry him alone into the silence without cracking my hands

beneath the bark, between the bars, into the hole, open like
a grave. And later we move away to a place where I've never
been, opening myself in front of him, a telescope kept in an
old shoebox, we see only a gray room without paintings or
corners. It's the dollhouse, you remember, out in the rain
there live three bears who do not sleep because someone may
be in one of their beds, who do not wake up because during
the day they had to find honey, before it hardened, and they
are tired.

52

IN THE AREA OF Navidad—Cardenal Caro Province in Region Six of the Liberator Bernardo O'Higgins—few locals have any desire to remember the summer of 1999. So, when questioned about the international event that took place in the neighboring town of Matanza, the residents look out to sea and murmur: Hmmm, yes, it was entertaining, there were so many gringos. I just did my thing, you know, I can't ignore my work, especially these days, everything's so hard. So I didn't see much. Like I've got the time to be worrying about some tourists. But yeah, I think a friend of mine had something to do with it.

The first time I traveled to the area, during the final months of 1999, I was disappointed not to find physical traces of the *Transensorial Beyond Seasons Celebration,* which I'd learned about from a television news program—the only one—investigating the disappearance of the Vivar siblings, before the coverage disappeared as quickly as they had. I thought that in Navidad and Matanza I'd find a trail left by the organization, propaganda on the walls, who knows, maybe some building that was built specifically for the event that had later been donated to the community. I searched wasteland areas, abandoned fruit stands, and at the municipal dump without luck for the detritus that, according to what I read in the international press, this transnational organization often left behind: posters, wax replicas of Hollywood actors, chicken carcasses without heads or extremities, jars of oil and acrylic paint, digital TVs, hair, overalls, suntan lotion, empty bottles, seaweed, used rolls of film, T-shirts and visors, burnt oil, stickers, lights, fast food wrappers, blankets, containers, colored lights, mirrors, plugs for American voltage, rubber gloves, tablecloths, Taiwanese cuddly toys, costumes of seventeenth-century French aristocracy, magazines, preservatives, exercise machines, microphones and headphones, sheets, holographic recordings, bicycles, beef jerky, unicycles and tricycles, dry leaves, towels, Styrofoam, bins of Panamanian fruit and vegetables, computers with biological processors, large white shirts, novels from every age in eight different languages, syringes, rackets, clay, encyclopedias, balls for various sports, fossils, hovercrafts, soaps, shampoos, DVDs and CD-ROMs, fetuses, straps and belts, couches, tons of tofu, folding parchment screens, car parts, bags of chalk, dozens of Catholic and Protestant Bibles, copies of Enuma Elish, Korans, Angas, Vedic books, Popol Vuhs, Mormon books, Tanajas, books of the origin of the Sikhs, Mishnas, books of Chilam Balam, Tao Te Chings, Talmuds, Bhagavad Gitas, Dhammapadas, Confucionist books, Kijikis, Nihongis, Tibetan and Egyptian Books of the Dead, Engishikis, Upanishads, books of Urantia, triptychs, eddas; kilos and kilos of sand.

I asked more than thirty locals what they remembered about the previous summer, and invariably they told me about their families or about the lack of opportunities in the province, and sent me to some neighbor who may have been involved in the event. Finally, at a service station, strategically located between the towns, the attendant—a man of forty-some years, who preferred not to make his identity public—told me that, although he wasn't directly involved with the organization (as his friend had said), he'd gone to "the mobile party" four nights in a row, where he worked as an assistant to a Chilean-African musician who played "a peculiar instrument." Or at least he thought the instrument was peculiar—he told me, later, sitting in the service station's cafeteria—because the sound it made was so sharp that it made something move in the pit of his stomach, like being tickled. Except for the last time, because he was too furious, he said with a smile, anticipating my series of questions. The instrument in question was the theremin of the Congolese Patrice Dounn, the other identity of the man I prefer to call Boris Real.

53

I SPENT THREE afternoons in January of 2000 sitting in a plexiglas booth, just over three feet wide, at a gas station between Navidad and Matanza. Behind me, there was a list of prices written in marker across the transparent surface and, above my head, there were products with brand names I thought had disappeared in Chile: Hilton Lights, Survivor, Pacific, Colo-Colo, Jockey Club, Ari, Nevada, Balu, Control. It was the only place I could sit and wait for the service station attendant. Every now and then some cars would pass by on the highway. The man wore a yellow jumpsuit and spent his time humming unintelligible music, alternating his activities between the broom, the ticket counter, and the oily floor of the mechanic's garage. At two in the afternoon, with a cheap book in his hand, he went to eat lunch in Navidad. The service station was left inexplicably vacant. At three the man came back, marked his time sheet and slid underneath a dusty Volvo that was parked in the garage. At one point, I thought I heard him snoring.

He enjoyed his job, he told me later, after the first beer. That first day I showed up at one in the afternoon, turned on my tape recorder and began to question him about Boris Real. He looked at me with surprise and said nothing. A fat man in a straw hat arrived in an oil truck, he greeted the attendant and asked him to fill the tank, then he left. A couple minutes went by and I didn't know whether to say something or to leave. A thrush landed a few meters away, it hopped around, jerked its head nervously, pecked at the ground. The man watched the movements of the bird. It hopped twice more and flew away. Only then did he speak to me: Not yet, *gancho*, wait till I get off, and buy me a beer. Then I'll answer you, can't you see I'm working. I asked him what time he'd be done with work and he replied that it depended on the traffic. During the middle of the week it was hard to know how many vehicles would pass by, he added.

That first day, waiting for him in that plexiglas booth, I picked up and read the book he'd taken with him at his lunch hour. The title was *James Versus the Spider,* a strange novel—horribly translated—whose premise postulated that in reality James Dean hadn't died in his famous accident, but that he'd ended up in a coma. Years later, for an exorbitant sum, his relatives auctioned off the unconscious body of the actor, selling it to a private clinic in Salt Lake

City. In secret, the clinic began a series of genetic experiments paid for by large pharmaceutical laboratories. The novel ended when the scientists failed in their DNA calculations and instead of cloning the perfect human being—beautiful, astute, sensitive, intelligent—they gave life to a tiny spider which was inserted, through the nose, into the president of the most powerful communications network in the United States, to feed on his brain and to direct the fate of the planet.

At sunset, in my car heading to the bar located on Matanza's small square, I asked the man from the service station where he'd bought that strange novel. A woman gave it to me, man. He was referring to a friend, or maybe a lover. We passed a few more minutes in silence. Then, to my surprise, he added: She loved to say that our friendship was just like that story.

56

DURING THE SUMMER we traversed the beaches of Chile's central coast in the Cadillac or the Porsche. I'd stop in a beach's parking lot and Bruno would get out of the car while I reclined in the drivers seat, shut my eyes and with closed lips sat humming old songs. I remember that we argued: Memory is made of music, he said; Memory is made of names, I maintained. I lay there with closed eyes, taking a drag on my cigar every now and then. That was the only movement alerting someone watching from outside that I wasn't sleeping. Sometimes I sat up, searching for Bruno among the swimmers. Then I'd guess, with a glance, which girl he'd chosen that afternoon.

58

ACCORDING TO WITNESS reports, Bruno Vivar would dive into the sea alongside various young women. He'd tell them a charming joke, pretend to drown or swim out a ways commenting on the size of an approaching wave, until one of the girls took the bait. Violeta Drago (27) tells how one afternoon in January of 2001 she saw a boy's body floating in the surf. It was a cloudy morning on the small beach of Algarrobo, only a few people felt inspired to go in the water. More confused than afraid, she says, she swam toward the body and took it by the waist to pull it back to solid ground. But when she touched it she knew immediately that it was a prank. There in front of the amazed girl, the inanimate body began to move. Bruno lifted his head from the water and smiled at the young woman. I'm cold, he said to her. Then it began to rain. Violeta left him there and swam furiously back to the beach. Those features, childlike and blue with cold, corresponded to the description of Bruno Vivar. His face was contorted, gaunt, says Violeta. If he was trying to act like a corpse, he very nearly succeeded.

59

THE BAR *MIRIADA*—just like that, without an accent mark—sits on Matanza's small square, next door to Don Julio's butcher shop, on the only urbanized block in town. Before I sat down, I paused for a minute, staring at the name written on a brass sign above the door. As a joke, I asked the man from the service station—who had come along, and was willing to answer my questions about Boris

Real, on the condition that I bought the beers—if *Miriada* referred to the bar's owner, assuming it was another orthographical error to be added to my list of provincial oddities: *miriada* for *miríada*, in other words: myriad, numberless, legion, quantity, abundance, infinity, plethora, excess. Maybe *Miriada* was the wife of Don Julio, the mother of Julito, or maybe it was the name of a waitress who'd broken his heart. No, said the waitress, who brought four liter bottles of Cristal pilsner for my guest and a brandy with gin and ginger ale for me. There's no one named *Miriada* here. It's what we call the tiny worms that eat the ears of corn, added the man from the service station. The trees used to be full of *miriada* in August, right at the end of winter. That's where the name comes from. Used to be, before what? I asked. Before the gringos showed up with their laboratories.

I pretended not to know which gringos he meant. It's fine, the man told me, wiping away the foam that had fallen from his lips. Do you want to ask me questions or just chat? We can talk about the African musician or about gringos, you decide, I have to work tomorrow and I can't spend all night drinking, I've got someone waiting for me at home: TV and a book. There would be enough time to inquire about the organizers of the "mobile party," I thought. Under the table, in a pocket of my bag, I pressed the button on the tape recorder, and told him that I didn't want to be a bother.

During the months of January and February of 1999 the locals had a lot of free time on their hands because the organizers of the *Transensorial Beyond Seasons Festival* had gotten the city council of Navidad and Matanza, in exchange for generous compensation, to suspend all commercial, civic, and social activity. The idea was to avoid all competition and consolidate control of the towns, forcing everyone to use the corporate logo of the international organization. In practice this meant that the restaurant on the fisherman's cove became part of a *fast seafood* chain; the bars and diners temporarily turned into pubs, taverns, cafés, tearooms, cabarets, trattorias, food courts, cafeterias, wine shops, lounges, casinos; and the service station, among many transformations, became a *Gas Station*. So the man spent those days sitting on a stump across the highway from the service station where he'd worked for so long. Accustomed as he was to spending his days in that place, he just sat and watched as massive tanks, and engines, and generators arrived. I like my job and I didn't want to be put out like that without getting to see why, he said. Every now and then a foreigner dressed in yellow and green overalls would approach him and attempt, in his words, to frighten him. But he just sat there, not understanding the language, until they left him in peace.

After a week of this routine, a convertible appeared on the highway. It was a small jewel, a collector's item—said the man from the service station—even though by then every kind of vehicle had already arrived and none would've surprised him. One time the ground even shook when a huge truck pulled up hauling a military tank, and then another one transporting several ATVs that had no wheels, they looked like rubber caterpillars. The man from the service station would've quickly forgotten the Porsche Spyder if it hadn't slowed down and stopped in front of him. Before the smiling and suntanned man driving could finish asking him, ridiculously, where he could find a service station, the Spyder shuddered and died. *Merde*—exclaimed the Congolese. Just what I need: *en panne*. Where can I get fuel? Maneuvering around obstacles, they pushed the car two kilometers to the man from the service station's home.

They arrived at nightfall. The foreigner was so tired that he fell asleep sitting up, at a chair in the kitchen while spooning sugar into his coffee. Oddly, though he was snoring, he never let go of the case that contained his musical instrument.

They got acquainted while pushing the Spyder, under the pleasant sun of that early summer evening. Dounn told the man from the service station that he'd driven all the way from Miami, he was in a hurry, and he needed an assistant to organize his performance with the Johannesburg Philharmonic Orchestra in three days' time.

60

THE MAN FROM THE service station allowed Patrice Dounn—alias Boris Real, alias Francisco Virditti—to stay in his house, in exchange for a little cash, after finding him asleep at the kitchen table. The Congolese had spilled the sugar. He stood up and began talking, in good Spanish, about money and the long hours he'd spent driving. At no point did he realize that his cheek and the right side of his forehead were coated with grains of sugar, nor that the impression of the plastic tablecloth was stamped on his right hand. He asked which room he should take and then disappeared with his luggage down the hallway. While he was preparing some food, the man from the service station heard his guest talking on a cell phone. It's not that I like to eavesdrop, he assured me, but my house is made of wood, and I was living alone at the time, so I was used to hearing everything.

After more than an hour, Dounn reappeared in the kitchen. He was more composed: dressed in a very elegant dark suit, his hair gelled, and his instrument case in one hand. He tasted the plate of rice with clams and Swiss chard that the man offered him along with a glass of boxed wine. He found everything "very tasty." Toward the end of the meal, he asked his host to turn down the volume on the television and inquired who lived in the other rooms. No one, replied the man. Before his mother died, the house had been a hostel. After her passing, he explained, he hadn't wanted any more kind-faced strangers in his house, so he closed the business. Now he had four guest bedrooms. Two matrimonial suites, one narrow bunk bed, and two twin beds. Dounn asked him if he'd be interested in accommodating some of his friends—a family—who were also coming to the festival that weekend. A couple and their two adolescent children. The man from the service station agreed, he needed the money. The Vivar family would be there in half an hour. Later the owner of the house would discover that the Congolese was very precise with his words: he'd only "accommodate" them, whatever that meant, because the Vivar's kept their luggage at the Royal Lethargy Grand Hotel and also slept—at least the parents did—in the executive suite they'd reserved there.

After he ate and finished off another glass of boxed wine that the man from the service station had offered him, Patrice Dounn proceeded to clear the kitchen table. Diligently he washed the dirty plates, glasses, and silverware, and cleared away the other things: the cruet, a journal of universal history that his host was reading, his own cell phone. He even removed the plastic tablecloth, which he folded neatly and placed in a corner of the kitchen. On the clean table he set down the black instrument case. He'd begun to open the clasps when suddenly he stopped and looked at the man from the service station, who was watching him from the door, a cigarette between his fingers. For the first time he understood how spiders and insects feel when someone observes them before stepping on them. That's how don Patrice looked at me, he said. He maintained eye contact for a few seconds until he could no longer stand it. He went into the hallway, asking the foreigner if something was wrong. Nothing, said Dounn, I just want to know if I can trust you. Yes, of course, whatever you need, was the host's reply. Then the Congolese added: This goes with you to the grave, understand? And he opened the case.

Inside there was no instrument. Just small cans made of a thin material, without label, arranged vertically. Dozens of cans. The host—maybe instinctively, he didn't know—hurriedly dug through a drawer of knives to find a can opener for the visitor. Then he left the kitchen, heading to the bathroom. He wasn't feeling well.

When he came back, both Patrice Dounn and his case had disappeared. He didn't see any sign in the garbage of the can that'd been opened, judging by the can opener—washed and dried meticulously, although still damp—sparkling on the table. The door to the guest's bedroom was closed. Again the man from the service station felt "fear in my gut and in my eyes and my hair. I'm telling you, my hair was standing on end. But then the urge to vomit passed, and I wanted to run, to head to the beach, to chase after women, or dance to a slow song."

But he never managed to do anything, because suddenly he heard someone pounding forcefully on the front door. It was the foreigner's friends. They were upset because they'd spent more than ten minutes calling and no one had come out to greet them. "One lady, one gentlemen, and two teenagers, they seemed to have been arguing among themselves. They were constantly interrupting each other, even the little girl would aggressively grab her father's shoulder every time she wanted to say something." They explained to him that they'd already spent two days in Navidad and that they wouldn't be spending the night at his house, although of course he'd be compensated. They were counting, however, on his discretion, the gentlemen told him in a low voice, while taking his hand for a second. When he withdrew his hand, in his palm, the man from the service station found a twenty-dollar bill. They asked about Dounn. The man said he didn't know, that he'd disappeared unexpectedly. Then they got back into a luxury Japanese sedan and left. Only Elena, Juan Francisco, and Bruno. When he went back into the house the man from the service station found Alicia sitting on his living room floor, looking through the book he was reading at the time. Always science fiction, really cheap editions that he bought in Pichilemu, he told me. How boring, said Alicia, and she asked what his name was. Then she wanted to know about his job and if he had any children. The girl took a cigarette from the pack that he had in the kitchen and put it in her mouth. The man offered her a light. Alicia made a noise, her tongue against her teeth. She said she didn't smoke, that he should leave her alone. Please, tell me where the beach is, I can't find it.

The man from the service station accompanied Alicia to the beach, walking two steps behind her for several kilometers through the night. She asked many questions and he answered them, aware all the time of the cash he'd make housing this strange group of people for a few days. Afterward everything would be calm and normal again. That's what he believed, he said. But it wasn't so. Every once in a while the girl would yell: Right? Left? And now, which way? It was like she was walking with her eyes closed, like she wanted to be guided in the darkness. Then all of a sudden the sound of the sea was very near. When the sand and *docas* came into view, Alicia started to run. Rising up from down below he heard a shrill, sharp sound. At first it seemed to him that a woman was screaming. Then he thought someone was doing something bad to the young girl. He quickened his pace across the beach. The night was moonless, and there were no streetlamps in the town, and so he was barely able to make out two distant silhouettes approaching the water. Little by little the shrill sound turned into a birdsong, into the gurgle of an immense stomach, and finally into a strange music. "A female robot, singing with her mouth shut in the shower," that's how Patrice Dounn's theremin sounded to the man from the service station. The foreigner was standing on a dune, an open case beside him—a different case, not the one he'd opened in the kitchen—his left hand suspended above a strange gleaming, blue instrument. The other hand, the right hand, moved slowly toward and away from the object. The music was very beautiful.

The man from the service station sat down to listen a few feet away. Soon, a third sound rose through the noise of the ocean and the song of the theremin. It was the voice of Alicia Vivar, who'd sat down silently next to the man from the service station. Resting her head on his arm she stared up at the stars. She hummed the melody that Dounn's instrument was playing, while at the same time, with a finger, she drew concentric circles in the damp sand, each one larger than the last.

Finally they were quiet, Alicia and the theremin. For a moment there was silence, "because the sound of the sea doesn't exist for those who live near it," said the man. Then the girl told him to look out at the waves. Patrice Dounn had begun to play another song. This is my favorite, "La Mer," by Debussy, Alicia whispered. Then she stood up and ran to embrace the Congolese.

65

DURING ONE OF MANY calm Sunday afternoon conversations in Sabado's white bedroom, I looked up from the computer screen, where I was reviewing her chapter of the novel-game, and spoke. What I'm going to tell you is a secret: when I was young I loved that song from *The Sound of Music,* called "My Favorite Things": *Raindrops on roses and whiskers on kittens, bright copper kettles, lalala-lala.* She smiled. I continued. I've always liked inventories, *Je me souviens* by Perec, or that other essay by Barthes where he lists his tastes. She said to me: That's true, inventories are beautiful when making them isn't obligatory. Above all I like lists as a literary form. She looked me in the eyes and added: Now, imagine a man, a theft, the murmur of the sea, the sound of people playing paddleball, the cry of seagulls, the playful flirtation of a man and a woman who are dodging the waves, a man and woman who at the same time sit down in the shade of a dune to look at some photographs. Does it say somewhere that our lives should be uncomfortable? Yes. The world. The rock. The sand. The sun.

Imagine then that the first man stole some towels. That he began running toward the dunes. That he heard the shouts of people behind him, the lifeguard's whistle. Get the thief, Get the thief. Someone tried to stop him by throwing a paddleball racquet at his legs. The impact of the wood against his shins hurt, but he kept running. Speed. There were many things he wanted to think about as he ran, clutching the new towels in his arms, but all he felt was the sand burning the soles of his feet. Through his mind flashed an evening in a campsite when Boris had taught them that to avoid being burned you had to focus your attention on the foot that cooled for an instant as it lifted up into the air away from the heat. He looked toward the end of the beach, past the dunes, where she'd be waiting for him, tan, half-naked, behind her dark sunglasses, the keys to the Spyder hanging from the tip of her erect ring finger. He yelled to her: Come on Alicia, run. The girl ignored him; she kept looking at the photographs and talking with her friend. And why should she respond? Her name wasn't Alicia. By the third shout, he was right in front of her, and she realized something odd was going on. She handed the photos to her friend, who sat beside her staring at the sea. She stood up and looked directly into the eyes of the man, who was gasping, covered in sweat. Before he could say anything, three policemen were dragging him toward a squad car. The towels were left behind, abandoned, there, at her feet. Sabado had to stop because it was getting late and I had to leave.

As we walked to the door, she told me how much she liked reading and writing in the novel-game. Everything is good; it's decaying, it's the image of a world destined to die and rot, and we're participating in the construction of that image. For what? For God? The truth, I replied, is that when we planned all of this with Viernes, at no point did we consider the comforts we'd leave behind. Excuse me, but what exactly do you mean by comforts?

71

THAT FIRST NIGHT, the wind blew ferociously on the beach in Matanza. The man from the service station told me that although his eyes filled with sand, he could still see Patrice Dounn, standing, playing his theremin—the sound of the instrument reverberated wonderfully in open spaces, the Congolese would tell him later—and at his side Alicia, lying on her back looking up. He couldn't tell if she was sleeping or staring at the stars. It was late, the wind was growing violent, and the man decided to go home.

Early that morning he woke up, shaken out of bed by a tremor. For some reason, the man from the service station described in great detail what he'd been dreaming that night, during the internal cracking of the earth, before seismic shudders threw him out of bed. In his dream, Navidad was a large modern capital, extensive and full of neon lights, futuristically designed automobiles, and a multiracial population. He was walking the streets of the city toward his wife's office, because she'd promised him that they'd go out to lunch. His wife was Alicia, the Vivar's young daughter. Then everything began to break. The man returned instinctively to the beach, shouting, terrified. The entire ocean had gathered into a huge wave, so tall its foam touched the clouds. Then he was soaking wet—the heat of the summer night in Navidad, he explained—walking through rubble of the city devastated by the enormous mass of water, and by the immense force of the current pulling it back. Concrete structures scattered everywhere, bodies of animals, entire parks pulled up by the roots, a dirty film covering all the useless objects, an unbearable, salty cold. He looked toward the place where Alicia Vivar's office used to be. He saw the building was intact, damaged, but standing, cut off from the rest of the city by a deep, wide chasm in whose depths he heard the echo of the ocean currents violently crashing against forgotten tectonic layers. Somehow he also heard Alicia's small voice desperately calling for him to get her out of there before the building collapsed. Then her voice was lost in the deafening rumble of the rising tide, as the ocean gathered again into a single enormous wave. An authority was shouting that if they wanted to survive they should climb the hills, climb to the highest places. The man started to run. He saw how everyone around him stumbled and fell, saw their terrified faces. Alicia's voice called his name with horrible desperation. She asked him not to leave her there; she didn't want to drown. Then the earth began to move violently. The man woke up afraid, bathed in sweat. He went to the door of his room, opened it, and stood under the lintel, waiting for the tremor to pass.

The clock on the living room wall showed six in the morning. He saw a delicate hand open the door of the room to his right. It was Alicia; she too was taking shelter in the doorway. Her hair was messy and her eyes barely open; she was wearing a red tracksuit under a large T-shirt featuring a Japanese anime character.

The shaking continued and didn't decrease in intensity; they waited for the jolt that at any moment would transform the tremor into an earthquake. Then the girl seemed to come awake, seeing the man a few meters away, watching her. She raised her hand in a friendly wave. The man from the service station murmured good morning. The tremor stopped.

As he moved toward the kitchen the man wiped his forehead with the back of his hand. He opened the refrigerator, took out a carton of milk and a jar of strawberry-colored powdered juice. He drank a glass and sat down at the small table. He stood up to turn on the television, but before he could he saw Alicia walking toward him and he sat back down, awkwardly. He offered her a glass of milk, which she accepted. The man asked about the foreign visitor. Alicia said: What do I know. She scrunched up her nose when she passed by him, muttering: Gross, you're all wet, like you just got back from the gym. And she sat down across from him.

He already had a couple liters of beer in his system and I think that's why the man from the service station told me all of this. Despite considering himself a fairly shy person—maybe because he was still kind of sleepy—he told Alicia about his dream. She listened with interest, getting up every now and then to look for sugar or a spoon, or to open a drawer and close it again, nervously. When the man finished telling her what he'd dreamed, she asked him if maybe he wanted her to be his *oneiromancer*. My what? Dream reader, like Joseph in Egypt. The man understood, he remembered that Joseph had gotten out of prison and become an advisor to the Pharaoh by revealing to him what God had been trying to tell him in a dream. At that point, the man from the service station inserted a small parenthetical to tell me that his father was an evangelist, and that when he was young, in Santiago, he'd frequently read him chapters from the book of Genesis before bedtime. He loved listening to those stories, but when his father would say goodnight and turn out the light, the shadows that came in from the street would keep him from sleep.

It was impossible to tell whether Alicia's offer was sincere or in jest. The man asked her how she knew about the biblical Joseph; outside the sun was coming up and they could hear the roosters crowing. The girl laughed and said that obviously she hadn't learned about it in her religion classes in high school. The man started toasting some bread. Alicia laughed again. She told him that his dream was simple: the sea was the world, parties, commerce. The city was the same. High places were high places. The sky. And her, why'd she make an appearance? Asked the man. At that moment they heard the honking of a car horn. The man and the girl looked out the window. In front of the house was parked the Japanese car of Juan Francisco Vivar. He was accompanied by his son Bruno and, asleep in the backseat, was Patrice Dounn.

75

I DIMLY remember what came next in the story told by the man from the service station that night at *Miriada*, in the town of Matanza. The truth is I'd finished three or four glasses of brandy, and he'd covered the table with more than a square meter of empty pilsner bottles. The light bulbs in the bar had faded gradually. Everything turned yellower, browner, blacker. Including the voice of my interlocutor. Still, I remember the dazzling young body of the waitress, who watched me out of the corner of her eye from another table, making calculations in a notebook. That's what I thought, with a total lack of intuition: the girl was making calculations. I'd only brought a ninety-minute tape, so by that point the conversation was empty air. Misleading human memory. The wind blew in through the cracks of a large, old window to my right. Progressively—mea culpa—the story of the disappearance of the Vivar siblings told by the temporary assistant of Patrice Dounn became, in my memory, a collage of blurry images. Without a doubt, the events that took place at the *Transensorial Beyond Seasons Celebration* were, in reality, much more impressive than how my alcohol-muddled mind recalls them.

That morning, Juan Francisco Vivar and his son made breakfast in the kitchen of the man from the service station. Patrice Dounn, half asleep, walked to his room and shut the door. Alicia went in with him, although after half an hour she came back out. She'd changed into a very thin green dress, her hair tied up with knitting needles. She sat down at the table. She drank chocolate milk and responded to a couple jokes Bruno made about the color of her outfit. Their father drank his coffee in silence without saying or doing anything. He just looked out the window. The man from the service station watched everything very nervously; it was difficult for him to understand the words the siblings spoke to one another. At one point, Juan Francisco stretched out his arm and pinched the soft flesh of his daughter's shoulder. Alicia didn't cry out or seem upset, according to the man from the service station. On the contrary, she tilted her head slightly as if it pleased her. Then Bruno and Alicia stood up at the same time and said they were going to the beach to go swimming. They retrieved two towels from the trunk of the car and left.

Even though it was cloudy, the man emphasized, the beach was full of tourists of all nationalities. This was apparent at first glance, in the varieties of hair and skin. It was the same burning sun, the same freezing sea, but all of a sudden one was no longer in Chile, in the same suffocating, monotonous summer as always, but on a gringo or European beach where everyone spoke loudly, where there were barely any children, and women were stretched out in the sun, their breasts in plain sight. They've told me that's how it is there, said the man. The beach of Babel, I remember remarking sarcastically, prompted by the biblical references he'd introduced into our conversation. The man from the service station laughed at this: Babel, yes. Just so. Asians, Islanders, Africans, Europeans, North and South Americans, everyone was speaking English. From what I was able to deduce from his description, the beach in Matanza was clearly divided into specific sectors—team sports, live music (classical, electronic, jazz, rock, indie, pop, and world music); artistic, recreational, and athletic dance; restaurants, bars, and kiosks; an ecological nudist zoo, water sports, libraries, virtual electronic games, spas, private security huts—marked off by buoys and plastic ribbons of the event's official color, a soft florescent white that at sunset turned into a metallic blue. Still, in the middle of invisible amplification systems, areas of acoustic isolation, and the roaring of passing motors, the occasional shouts of *"pan de huevo," "cuchufli, barquillo," "helado, helado, heladito," "lleve la palmera pa los regalones"* rose up from the town's local vendors, authorized by the organization to supply the event with local color.

That morning, Bruno and Alicia looked for the least crowded area to lay down their towels. The Swimmers Section, about eleven meters from the water, at the center of the beach. The best spot on any of the nation's beaches was deserted. The tourists preferred to lie down between the dunes, for more intimacy, or on the terraces of the restaurants or bars. The man from the service station arrived to the spot around three in the afternoon, carrying the theremin case, following Patrice Dounn. The Congolese was much more expressive with his music: I want to see the children, they're at the beach, take me . . . Don't lose my case. Those were the only words he'd uttered since appearing in the kitchen that morning, after having slept off what, the man from the service station suspected, was a hangover. But he was wrong. That man always had a hangover. The hangover of hate and fear, which is a type of boredom, he said. Without losing his composure, Patrice Dounn removed his Italian shoes and silk socks. He rolled up his suit pants so that later he'd be more comfortable on the damp white towel of Alicia Vivar, who, from the water, waved to them and gave a little shout. On his own towel, Bruno Vivar pretended to be sleeping, hiding his face in his forearm.

The man from the service station offered descriptions I'm unable to forget: Bruno, completely hairless and pale, tiny next to Patrice Dounn, dressed all in black, wearing sunglasses, his hair gelled. Without warning, the musician picked up some sand in his left hand, holding it up in the air, leaning his head slightly toward the boy. Anticipating what he was about to do, Bruno leapt to his feet. With both hands he grabbed Patrice Dounn's venomous fingers and made him open them, forcing him to drop the sand. You were going to throw sand at me, blurted Bruno. He grabbed a fistful and threw it at him. The fraudulent Congolese barely reacted as the sand struck him in the face; he spat modestly and tried to smile. Poor boy, he murmured. There followed a conversation in English that the man from the service station couldn't understand.

A while later, señor and señora Vivar arrived. It was about six in the evening, the heat had increased and the guests of the *Transensorial Celebration* covered the beach. Alicia was still in the water. Her brother, father, and Patrice Dounn were conversing in some language that, if it wasn't English, must've been French. All three were lying motionless on the sand, looking up at the blue sky through black sunglasses. Teresa Elena Virditti, señora Vivar, was reading a magazine, indifferently. After flipping through the pages once or twice she looked up at the man from the service station, who was watching her daughter swimming in the sea. Curiously she asked him how long Alicia had been in the water. The man told me that he'd wanted to say: How would I know? I'm not your nanny. But instead he said: About four or five hours. Señora Vivar looked at her watch. She shook her head saying the girl was very irresponsible, she'd end up catching a cold and, of course, she'd have to spend the whole next day at her bedside, worrying over thermometers and remedies. She was very cynical, said the man from the service station. Like they didn't have tons of employees who'd take care of Alicia. At that point, after the brandy in the bar had run out and I'd begun to drink my companion's beer to stay animated, I wondered to myself about the relationship between the man from the service station and Alicia Vivar. Why he paid so much attention to a preadolescent; how he knew so much about the life of that family; why he seemed to particularly detest Juan Francisco and Elena. I didn't want to interrupt his story by asking these questions. Or maybe these questions could just as easily have been directed at myself, at the motivation behind this story.

As the afternoon light waned and the color of the signs and the organization's emblems changed slowly to the aforementioned electric blue, the beach was suddenly overrun with street vendors. The same ones who, during the day, had been offering the *cuchufli*, the *palmera*, the *mote con huesillo*, the *pan de huevo*, or the *mani tostado*, were now dressed in T-shirts and hats with the official logo of the *Transensorial Celebration*. It was then that Teresa Elena Virditti ordered the man from the service station to go tell Alicia to get out of the water because she was going to catch a cold. The man from the service station instinctively responded, "Yes, señora," although he didn't stand up, but waited until Patrice Dounn looked at him and nodded his head. In the end, it was the Congolese who paid him, he told me. He went toward the water navigating around the foreign couples, stretched out on the sand. He observed that each one of them was receiving a gift from the street vendors; it looked like one or two cans of that already familiar, strangely glowing, beverage, which the tourists received with delight: immediately opening the cans and drinking the contents. He'd watched this scene the previous day (the foreigner anxiously opening the same can), and he wondered what it was. It's hadón, Alicia shouted to him from the water.

There were almost no swimmers left, they'd all gone back to the beach to receive their dose of hadón. Only the man from the service station and Alicia were in the water. He tried to speak to her, but the girl pretended not to hear and swam out into the waves. Once they were out far enough that no one could see them and no wave would break over them, Alicia stopped and told him "a few of the most sordid family stories" that the man had ever heard. He told me that the girl was very sad, very lonely. When she began to cry she dove underwater and then came back up smiling. I interrupted the man from the service station to ask him what he meant by "sordid stories." I'd prefer not to get into the details, he responded, because it wasn't his business, it was hers. She'd grown up now and had moved on.

How was he so sure, I insisted. The man just smiled. Then he said that after many years of living on the coast, he believed he knew the sea well. He'd swum in the early morning and swum for entire afternoons. He'd even gone out in the bay with fishermen, during the winter, when it was raining and everything. But he'd never seen a sunset from high sea. It's definitely special, he said. It sounded corny and something else, I thought. Rewriting this I come up with this idea: in love. The two of them were admiring how the circle of fire slipped into the water, he told me, when Alicia said desperately that she didn't know what she was going to do with her life. She'd stopped going to mass, but the priests said nothing. She treated anyone who wanted to be her friend badly and no one asked her why. She'd skipped classes so many times, no one cared. She tried insulting her teachers so they'd expel her from school, but nothing happened. She tried going to parties that went on for days, drinking herself into a coma, smoking so much marijuana that she forgot her brother's name. It was all so boring and mediocre, she said. Nobody danced well. Nobody even sang properly. She knew exactly how every movie she went to would end, every book she read. She couldn't stand men, except Bruno and Boris, she told him, both of whom she loved madly. At this point, the man from the service station didn't even try to explain to me who this Boris was who'd suddenly appeared in his story. He must've seen in my face that I already knew half of it. Alicia couldn't stop crying. Relax, you're only fourteen, the man tried to calm her as they swam back toward the beach. Hearing this, the girl swallowed her sobs and looked at him disdainfully. That's just it, I don't know what else to escape from. I can't stand myself because I'm part of them, of the ones I hate, she said, pointing with her chin toward the Vivars.

By then they could touch the ocean floor. Hurrying to finish his last beer—it was already four in the morning—the man lowered his voice: Then I advised her to do something without realizing I was doing it—run away from her parents.

It was getting dark. They didn't notice that a big wave was approaching and it broke over them; in the confusion, the girl hugged the man underwater, and he—instinctively, he assured me, like that excused it—also wrapped his arms around her. They came out onto the beach half-drowned, and moved furtively to the rocks, then walked to the dirt paths, and the interior fields of Cardenal Caro. First they went to the man's house in Navidad, taking one suitcase and a large sum of money from Patrice Dounn's room. Making sure no one saw them leave the town together, they met at a bus stop on the southbound highway, where they boarded the first bus that passed by.

They were happy, and scared because of what they'd seen on the beach in the moment of their flight: the foreigners were screaming insults at the sky, their eyes swollen in fury. A few had taken off their clothes and were running toward the town, hunched over and howling. Others bashed their heads against posts. Many ran over whomever was in front of them. The same scene was repeated everywhere: a man would pull a women's hair and she'd defend herself by throwing sand in his eyes, then the man would throw a fistful at her, and she'd jump on him and scratch his back. The same thing, over and over.

The spectacle of a crowd, violent and blind—eyes open, but unseeing—didn't appear to be part of the organization's plan. The last thing he saw, said the man from the service station, were a dozen helicopters landing on the beach. Hundreds of security guards from the organization fell on the maniacal tourists; they carried syringes with a strange purple liquid. Juan Francisco and Elena Vivar were scratching at each other just like everyone else until they were tranquilized by the injection. It's just a blood transfusion, Alicia told him on the bus, before falling asleep. And I think it was then that the man from the service station stopped speaking. He lit a cigarette and stared out the large window at the small plaza of Matanza. I've got to go to the bathroom, he muttered. The waitress sighed. Then she closed the notebook and said to me, though I didn't anticipate her intervention: hadón is a drug whose effects are only mitigated by the blood of other people. I turned and looked at her attentively. Hate, fear, she began to pronounce with emphasis. Only perfect love dispels fear, she quoted. Before the man returned from the bathroom, I already knew that the waitress was Alicia Vivar.

80

Two photographs.

Out of the stack she gave me before walking away as one possessed, two of the photographs would have distinct destinies yet also the same one. Before forgetting the sea and diving into the photos, I felt as if my emotions were abandoning me. Strange, in the same way people abandoned this beach at nightfall, heading toward their cabanas, to the hotel, to houses, with damp sand between their toes, with low blood pressure and a faraway longing, like the murmur of the sea. Like waves. Feelings as subjects, like people who come and go. I imagined myself stretching out on the sand, looking up, the photographs scattered on my towel, empty though not unfeeling. This last phrase I associate with two very important people, although with affects of distinct nature: in the novel-game I called them Sabado and Viernes. They both gave up, they both decided not to finish it, but there was no fear in them, just the opposite. Or is it the same thing? Desire, need—need twisted underground and turned into a tree whose branches shelter us from the sun—such that we, the remaining participants in the novel-game, longed to wake up beside them one morning, and have time and sufficient light to contemplate their unprotected faces up close. She (Sabado) would be laziness, he (Viernes), competence. I heard footsteps on the sand: my feelings moved off toward the police station. I tried to go back to the novel-game: Alicia would be happy that she was the owner of the towels and that it was all a misunderstanding. B was still free, they were meeting in the hallway, they looked each other in the eyes, searching for what they liked in each other's faces. Is this to see? This is not why we were given eyes. I felt a desire to kiss someone, as if I'd not done so in a long time. Empty. I sat down on her towel to look at the photos. And what I saw were not images I could attribute to Boris Real, to the journalist, or to Domingo—not even to that two-faced character who comingles them—rather it was I, Carlos Labbé, who had them in my memory.

In the first one I'm with my grandmother and my brother in Matanza, in the area of the beach where tourists typically take keepsake photos. It was probably my father who took it. He was always taking photos at the time, but, as he got older, he lost that urgent need to keep a family album. There's a narrow white border on the photo paper. Our attention, mine and my brother's, has always been drawn to the clothes we were wearing: everything covered in stripes, leather sandals that we hated because we thought they looked like women's sandals. And we were holding hands, with bright smiles. My grandmother looks so young, sixty-something, I guess. She's smiling too, the same smile as always. I'm six and my brother is eight, yes, we're holding hands. The sea is cool, my mother would've been watching from a distance, no longer moved because raising us had become habit for her. Could it be possible? I have a wide forehead, like an old man, my eyes already hidden. My brother was everything I wanted to be: his clothes, his voice, his bicycle (which really belonged to me because I won it in a drawing contest in Provida, but it was too big for me so they gave it to him), his women. It was a time of complete silence, of a white cat in my arms, of hundreds of Legos on the rug, of a deep longing for things of unfathomable dimensions, of absolute obedience to God because I was terrified of what my classmates might do to me if the opposing team made a goal. I played defense because I was bad at everything sports related. On the other hand, I was good at drawing. An inexplicable shiver passed through my entire body (I've almost never experienced a pleasure so intense) when we traveled to Rancagua or San Bernardo and I, from the left window in the car's backseat, associated the colossal image of water towers bordering the highway with the smell of butter I discovered when I licked the open palm of my hand. This photo would end up, as you might imagine, on the wall at the back of my grandmother's apartment, in the corner of a collage one of my aunts made with photos of all the grandkids from Easter or a birthday.

The second photo is a close-up of six, smiling adolescent faces, insecure but acting like they could handle any situation. At least that's my expression. Owing to the lack of details—decorations, objects, even clothes—the photo could be from the present day. The date is "December, 1991." We're in the room I shared with my brother, in La Isla, the property we lived on near Rancagua. Undeniably we're adolescents. In the photo are some friends from Nogales, a neighborhood of country houses, which today is an exclusive residential condominium. My brother—who was always in charge of where we went, why, and when—took the photo. El Coco, with a slender face and no pimples, smiled openly because someone must've said something funny. He was an insufferable snitch and at the same time cared for you. He was the first of us to swim down the fastest moving branch of the river. He was pretty and covered with hair; the women loved him. El Muno, blonde, small and clever, spoke little, and seemed not to care about people. He'd invented a language for himself, he smoked sticks that we found in the river, he drank alone, he read a lot, he'd spent a delightful evening—according to him—two summers ago with a female cousin from Australia. He was obsessed with masturbation. El Muno was a liar. He lived in a world he'd invented. He let Chep and I in, but only as his servants. I, like everyone, was attracted to his sister Quela, so I always wanted to go over to his house. Now anything I say about Yel, Chep, and Tomas—brothers separated from each other by one year, whom we called the Monkeys—will always be insufficient and inexpressive. In the photo, Yel has lots of pimples. Yel built clubhouses, put together shelves for his room, fixed radios. He was a monster. He covered us with loogies. He liked to hump his brother's friends and we couldn't do anything about it because he was tall and violent. But if you were alone with him he was nice, he asked you things an older brother would ask. He was responsible. Today—married of course, bald, a successful architect—he treats me with great kindness, but still calls me a horrible nickname that has to do with excrement. Chep was, and maybe still is, my best friend. We were about the same age and he liked to talk, drink coffee, and smoke a little bit. He's blonde with a big face, like Felipe from *Mafalda*, with a gap between his front teeth so big he could spit through it. He's extremely sentimental, he can't regulate his emotions, every now and then he'd invent alternate personalities with outlandish names: Chichimau, Yoduca-estan-de-casafala, The Ambilibiboy, Pato Yanez, Simioldi, Tribilin, The Pastam, and other beings I've forgotten. Once we were walking to his house at night and he said to me, trembling, that he couldn't see anything, that he'd gone blind. Seriously. He always did things like that, and I'm gullible. I led him by the arm through the night, careful now there's a pothole, to the right there's lots of mud, Chep, what's wrong, Chep. And then? We were entering his house. Coming in through the front door and he started to laugh—I think he might have kept on laughing his whole life—at my worried expression. He liked mowing the lawn at his house, watching television, making home videos with his video camera, changing the lyrics to famous songs, repeating jokes until they were worn out, and playing soccer. Also he was afraid of being rejected by women and of sex, above all. He was clumsy; he was hard working. He could vomit at will. On Sunday mornings when he woke up he'd run to his parent's bedroom, pick up his baby sister, and carry her to his bed, so he could sleep with her smell. I miss him. I've spent too much time locked in this laboratory.

In the photograph we'd just come back from the river, where we swam naked in December and January. Then, with mud up to our ears, we'd jump in the pool at my house to wash off. We made toast, spread butter on it, and walked back to the Monkeys' house, two kilometers down a dirt path. On the way we talked about fun things and laughed at the wimps—whose only representative, most of the time, was I. Today the photograph is lost in my parent's living room, in one of those awful cardboard albums that photo-processing labs give out. My sister loves looking through those albums when she's bored.

I dropped the photographs. I thought about the odd grammar Viernes used in his farewell email: I'm not even grateful that I have met you by chance. I realized that if I'd been lying on the sand at the beach all this time, I'd be cold. I stretched again. I saw the girl coming back toward me from the street. Her hair messy, she carried a bucket full of water, and one towel was hanging over her shoulder. God, how I love her. I think about all the names I've given her in all the things I've written. I also think about the emptiness here in my bedroom, without fear or hope, without ever having been touched by anyone, not even propositioned by anyone, except by Sabado; but she was drunk, that's another story and I wasn't myself. I gathered the photos into a pile. I prepared myself to stop searching, to stop searching for her. I know where I am—I said to myself as I stood up—when I imagine that nocturnal beach, immense, empty of human beings. I was wrong, all the same. The girl, the child—Alicia—had started to build sand castles on the beach. Anxiously I yelled to her: The tide is rising.

82

I STOOD UP QUICKLY and went over to the table where Alicia Vivar had been doodling with a pencil in a notebook with yellow pages. I looked into her eyes. Her childish face held my gaze with the kind of expression that precedes a sigh and tears, or an outburst of mocking laughter. She'd been present throughout my whole conversation with the man from the service station, in the *Miriada*; she didn't need an explanation. We'd slowly gotten drunk off of drinks she'd brought us and, as the night went on, while she replaced my empty glass with a full one, she'd been able to observe how both my general and specific questions about Boris Real, about hadón, about Juan Carlos Montes, about the *Transensorial Celebration,* and about the disappearance of the Vivar siblings might be summarized in a single, repeated question: And Alicia? And Alicia? And Alicia?

It was already early morning. Crickets and frogs competed to fill the space in the darkness—what in the city we call silence—with their songs. I reached out my hand and took her by the wrist. Alicia let the pencil fall and gave a little cry. I asked her: When? She said: Tomorrow, here. Her eyes left mine, focusing on something behind me. Was someone else there besides Alicia Vivar and myself? I turned around instinctively: I'd forgotten him. The man from the service station, drunk and furious. You will not take her, was the last thing I heard. Then an intense blue spark, like a short circuit in a place without electricity, and everything went black. I'm dead, I thought. But before that happened, I'd glimpsed the arm of the man from the service station drawing back so he could smash his fist into my face. I'm not dead, because I hurt, I told myself the next morning. I was in my car, at the service station, vomiting.

83

I WALKED TO THE service station, turned on the spigot, and drank and drank. My head throbbed so much I felt it belonged to somebody else. When I washed my face my cheek began to burn. I called to the man from the service station a few times, but no one was there. The highway was empty and the day cloudy. A bag was being carried slowly along by the breeze. I called out again in vain. Some sparrows flew toward the iron roof of the cigarette stand. The strange thing was that the vending machines were on and the chain that normally locked off access to the service station at night or during lunch hour was lying on the ground. Someone had brought me there, parked my car, and left without hurting me too badly or providing an explanation. Despite the fact that I knew what I knew about the disappearance of Alicia Vivar, neither the man from the service station, nor Boris Real, nor Juan Francisco Vivar, had taken advantage of my drunkenness to silence me. It was as if this individual wanted me to be healthy and safe in my car, ready to go write the story he'd told me. I got in the car, started the engine, and turned on the radio. An old American song, "Memories Are Made of This," was playing. I whistled along until the song ended. I thought about what the man from the service station had said the night before in the bar, as a truck went by at full speed on its way to San Fernando. On the radio, a woman's voice began to tell the news. It was two fifteen in the afternoon on the first day of March.

I realized that I still had the tape recorder. The tape was there too.

The assignment—or my whim, if you like—was finished: I could piece together what happened to the Vivars that summer day in 1999. The story would exemplify the double standard at the heart of appearances and disappearances of Chileans, but none of this sounded right to me. The dramatic effect was too perfect. The pieces fit with suspicious ease: the perverse executive, the hedonistic musician, the tormented nymphet, the international orgy, the mysterious drug. A love story about a provincial man and under-age girl from the capital. Then at last, I remembered Alicia Vivar's words: Tomorrow, here. I turned off the radio, started the car, and went back to Matanza.

I parked on one side of the small plaza. A bunch of kids were milling around in front of a man selling cotton candy. I figured it was the novelty of summer. I went into the *Miriada* looking for the apron that Alicia had been wearing the night before, but in her place I found a fifty-something-year-old manager, running a damp cloth across the surface of the bar. She asked me if I wanted breakfast. In the corner, two old men were disinterestedly watching a daytime television series, sucking down bowls of soup. I sat. I ordered a sandwich and a mineral water. After fifteen minutes, when the manager brought out paper napkins, mustard, and ketchup, I stared at her. I didn't know if I should talk to her about Alicia. Whether or not I'd be able to communicate with her. In the end, I asked her what time the younger waitress started working. The manager smiled and exclaimed: The womanizer has been bitten by a spider. A while later, as she brought me a coffee, I asked her directly about the waitress named Alicia. The woman was taken aback at my insistence. No waitresses work here, just me. Sometimes the old man, when he's not drinking.

The hangover had consumed my patience. I took out a bill, placed it on the table, and looked her in the eyes: Last night a woman named Alicia was working. One of the men in the corner stood up and leaned on the bar next to me. Last night *nothing*, insisted the woman. She was the only person who worked there, and she didn't have to explain herself to anyone. It'd be better if I just left; this was not a place to try and pick up women.

I walked out into the plaza. It was five in the afternoon; Matanza's infamous wind was blowing. I wanted to go back to my apartment in peace, forget about the Vivars, sleep calmly. In a couple of days the story would be written. The strange feelings would be forgotten. Once written, the truth about the parts played by Alicia and Boris Real would be reduced to those of characters in a book (or worse, in a journal), and Matanza and Navidad would become exotic towns on postcards from provincial Chile.

Before going back to Santiago—while buying a postcard that depicted a fisherman smiling on the cold, dry beach, under a white sky—I randomly overheard the conversation of a man working in the market and a woman, sitting on a wicker stool, weaving. The man told her that he'd finally be able to pay off a debt because he'd come into some unexpected money. A few days ago, while he was walking with Violeta on the beach toward the cove, "Boris" had approached him and asked if his daughter, who was shivering because she'd just come out of the water, would be interested in becoming an actress. How random, the woman said. Boris told him that at the school in Navidad they were going to be putting on a play at the beginning of the school year. And Violetita would be perfect for the part. Imagine that, Violetita an actress, said the woman indifferently.

I interrupted to ask the man where I could find this Boris. At the service station they both replied at the same time; the service station attendant is named Boris.

89

LITERATURE IS A LIE. Embrace the wind. Today is Saturday, the fourteenth day of September in the year two thousand and two since the birth of Jesus Christ. I'm sitting in front of the screen, the keyboard, and the speakers of my computer, at eight hours twenty minutes past noon, in an apartment in a building on Merced, whose number, with respect to the Plaza de Armas in Santiago de Chile, is four-hundred seventy-one. Twenty-five years have passed since my mother gave birth to me. More than twenty minutes ago a beautiful woman left my apartment, up from the armchair, out through the door into the hallway, and gone. Thirty minutes from now I'll be sitting in front of the television. Only what happens exists. Only what I can see, hear, touch, smell, taste. Nevertheless, she bit her bottom lip and smiled. She looked at the floor. I sensed for a brief instant the chess game of God. She'd been thinking about me too, and my body was attracted to hers like metal to a magnet. It is now, here. You might say that I want to raise walls, construct a bedroom, write a chapter in a novel where the two of us would touch each other freely. But I don't. She looks at the clock and says: I have to go.

It is a game. Not a novel.

There is no story. Only rules.

95

MARTES LET HIMSELF fall to the floor. His hands hurt and he was tired of thinking about ways of escaping. Surely Juan Carlos Montes had laughed seeing him running circles around the room and slamming into walls. He only hoped for two things: that Sabado was truly safe in a city somewhere, and that the message she'd sent him was a lie, a joke in bad taste devised by Domingo to frighten him. If Montes locked them together in a room, like the lab mice they were, the hadón would take effect and one of the two would end up killing the other. Which in itself would be useless, for the survivor would quickly be eliminated by Montes. At this point, he saw no way out but through the precarious lines of the novel-game that they began to write when there were still seven of them, like the days of the week.

99

DO YOU REMEMBER how many times we discussed that Wittgensteinian way of looking at things? And how many times we talked about idealism? That objects don't exist, dear Sabado, only words, which build and break, build and break. It's impossible to know what happens to the apple when you bite it. To write with hate. Under the effect of hadón, wanting my words not to bite the open chin, the purple cheek, the white eyes of Martes, but to bite your throat, your neck, your mouth, from a distance. Let me hate you,

Sabado, since I can't touch you, to dispel the death of these four walls. For this I write you.

"But tell me, do you hate me?" Martes asked me, before smashing his head against the wall of mirrors and falling unconscious to the floor. He's not dead; he sleeps, I believe. I hope.

The only way to save the head is to train it. In the Lacanian sense of the term, Montes would say, because, he claims, the mind is only language.

Or an invention of language.

I too let myself fall to the floor of the entertainment room, my hands locked together, staring at Martes. They've locked the door from outside, right? He asked me. He already knew. He'd read it in an email you sent him, he said. We'll kill each other beyond saving, Domingo. The compound should already be working in our hypothalamuses. Really I don't hate you, he continued, occasionally I've been bothered by your need to control everything, just a little bit. That you seemed indifferent to the disappearances of Viernes, Miercoles, Lunes, and Jueves. But tell me, do you hate me?

No, I replied. I continued to stare at the ceiling, humming a suite by Debussy that my father listened to on Sundays, early in the morning. La la la la. La la la la la. Do you remember "Le mer?" Jueves bought a theremin on the Internet and it arrived on a Saturday. It was the perfect excuse to celebrate. While we put peanuts in his beer, Jueves moved his hands toward and away from the apparatus. The terrifying sound waves oscillated from the deepest to the sharpest. Uuuuuuu, uuuuuuuuuuuuuuuu. I don't know. Jueves spent a couple weeks making sounds with it; he even printed the Debussy score. This must have been during the period when I was writing the story about the Congolese on the beach. You remember. It was a Friday night, we were playing cards. I got up to go to the bathroom and when I came back the chairs of Lunes, Miercoles, Jueves, and Viernes were empty.

"But, tell me, do you hate me?"

I stopped humming the suite when Martes's shouts grew more powerful than my own. I told him: I'm not going to kill you, I'm sorry. I believe in God, that God gives and takes life, and that if I do it intentionally, I'll be definitively separated from Him, which is the same as dying. Martes began kicking furniture and throwing papers in the air. Rage all you want, but don't touch the computer, I howled. I brandished the leg of a chair, ready to give him a real blow in the neck, below the nape to calm him. He sat down and kept screaming that I was a fool, a fool. Only a fool can believe in God while at the same time experimenting with cannibalistic white mice. I closed my eyes. I remembered that when Jueves's hands moved away from the theremin, the sounds were deeper. Martes continued. Shit on the angels, on the first, on the second, the third, the fourth, the fifth, the sixth, the seventh, shit on every single one of the days of creation. That's what he said. And he added the names of the patriarchs, of the judges, of the prophets, of the kings, of the King. So I stood up and I took the chair leg in my hands. I calculated where I should strike him so there'd be no blood. Right at that moment he stopped talking. He asked me if I hated him. He moved quickly to dodge my blow, his right leg tangled with what was left of the couch and his head smashed against the mirrored wall. He's unconscious now. Until someone kills him or revives him.

I remember it well. I came back to the entertainment room from the bathroom and there were four empty chairs. I thought they were pulling a prank. For the rest of the afternoon I opened every door, every closet, I looked under every bed. Nothing. Sabado and Martes were too busy to tell me if they'd seen the others leave. On the computer I wrote that Bruno and Boris Real had traversed the beaches of the central coast, so that later I could email that chapter to the others. While I was writing, I felt like I was walking the seaside streets of the novel. I was furious, as I am now. I've felt this way for a long time, ever since my mother took my brother to the supermarket and left me at home. Ever since I kissed a girl who I really liked; she moved her lips softly as if mouthing a phrase or a name. I backed away quickly and asked her what she was saying. I'm sorry, she whispered. A few days later I found out she was seeing someone else. There was someone following me when I left the market in Navidad. A little girl on roller-skates. She's been behind me for a while, I thought; she knows something. I stopped and she stopped. She was beautiful, I remember: she was about to go through puberty. I thought that her name must be Alicia or Violeta—a strong name, tinged with adventure. And that she must've seen the others leave the laboratory and run to the beach. The girl must have an important message. Alicia, tell me, where are they? Who? She asked with an expression of distrust. Please, can you get out of the way? I need to get past. And she was gone.

This is the end of the message, my dear. I am going to press send, I'll run circles around the room until I gather enough courage to smash my head against the mirror. I hope I don't die.

If I wake up, I hope I'm not alone.

100

THE BRILLIANT IDEA had been Bruno's. That afternoon, when the journalist showed up at the beach, the oldest Vivar had said: Now I know where we can get some cash. Then he looked his sister gravely in the eyes and she noticed his lips were smeared with sand. You're disgusting, Alicia said to him. He smiled and slid his hand under the towel.

It'd be simple: they were relying on the fact that after sixteen years, the journalist wouldn't have forgotten them.

He's a writer now, it might not matter to him what happened in the past or what stopped happening, murmured Alicia, sunning herself. Those are the bad writers, the ones who call themselves poets, her brother said, as he watched the man undress his little girl and put on her bathing suit. Alicia lowered her dark sunglasses and gave Bruno a glacial look: What're you trying to say? Well, you write poetry, you should know, replied Bruno. Disgusting, she repeated, and smiled. Better save that smile for the lovely interview that awaits you.

The next day, at five in the afternoon, Alicia got up off her towel. They'd spent the entire night inventing and disguising the sordid story that she'd tell the journalist. Why we ran away from our parents, who tied us to our cribs, and abused us. The more I cried the redder my father's face got and the more painful his blows. Or worse: they never even touched us. They wouldn't say our names. On weekends they locked us in the attic with bags of dog food, this is why the only living human I can tolerate is my brother; it's not that I love him. That's why we stole the Porsche and headed north: something eye-catching, bright, a toy for us and no one else. At Christmas they let us open presents, but only open them. Then they'd take the toy away and put it on a shelf, at a height we couldn't reach.

Alicia set down the book she was reading and wrapped her body in a thin blue dress. A few meters away the journalist was sitting on the wet sand, his legs stretched out in front of him. Every now and then the surf splashed the soles of his feet, which must've felt delicious, but the intent, serious expression never left his face. Except when the little girl came running toward him from the sea, where she was swimming with her mother, and yelled something to him. Then he smiled, although he didn't answer her. Just a smile.

Alicia started walking toward the journalist. Some vacationers were playing paddleball and the sounds of conversations mingling with the murmur of the sea, formed the same uniform mass of sound she'd heard so many summers throughout her life. She remembered a childhood afternoon in Zapallar, in her aunt and uncle's house. She was nine years old. After lunch she took her book and went alone down to the beach. She didn't sit on the sand, but on the grass between the parking lot and the shore. She sat there reading and watching people for hours, until the sun began to drop and she got hungry. Then she walked back to the house, always the same. Thinking about what she'd tell her mother when she asked the same questions as always ("Did you have a good time?" "Did you eat a lot of ice cream?" "Did you make a new friend?" "Did you wear sunscreen?"). Forgetting the answers because there was always something that distracted her. Once she found a cat that'd been hit by a car, lying on the pavement. It was in agony. Someone had had the decency to move it so that the cars passing by in the street wouldn't crush it. Surely this person, who'd carried it in their hands, must've realized that it was alive and had left it there anyway. Alicia remembered asking herself, feeling very sad, why such cruel people existed; it never occurred to her that apathy might be an explanation. She sat down next to the cat. It was gray with white and yellow spots, and a very fluffy tail. Its back—which was cut open—oozed a white, fetid liquid; it was bleeding from one ear, from the eyes, and the anus. Its left rear foot hung, connected to the body only by skin. She too was incapable of doing anything, except accompanying it while it died. She caressed its head and soon the cat began to purr. She couldn't swallow her tears. She also felt—for a moment—a desire to crush it with her foot or throw it in the street so the cars would obliterate it. She'd given it a name, Maximiliano. A name she liked a lot. Soon night came and the cat stopped purring. It breathed less frequently all the time, it was getting cold. Alicia decided that no, the cat wouldn't be called Maximiliano, because maybe someone else had already named him and it wasn't fair that he should spend his last moments with another name. And finally he died. That time she got home late. They scolded her. If she was going to be out walking at that hour then she wouldn't be allowed to go to the beach on her own. She told them about the cat and her mother yelled: That's why you smell so bad.

Alicia continued walking across the beach. The journalist was on his side, drawing pictures in the sand that his daughter finished with her tiny fingers. When she was just a few steps away from them, the surf came up and erased the drawing. The journalist lifted his head noticing her presence. His expression didn't change. Alicia sat down next to them. The daughter put a wet, sandy hand between them; in the middle of her palm a sand flea writhed. She asked if the flea would die if it stayed out of the water for a long time. The journalist replied that it wasn't water that it needed, but water and sand mixed together.

Alicia wanted to add something to his answer. She remembered when she was young she'd kept a few fleas in a jar, with seawater and sand and everything, and that still, the next day they were dead. She opened her mouth but didn't say anything. The journalist sat looking at her. In that moment she should've begun telling him about the Vivar family, about her childhood, about Boris Real, the longing, Bruno, her father's chemistry laboratory, the woman, the sirens, the hadón, the bloodless body of James Dean that'd given her nightmares until she was thirteen; yet all three of them sat in silence. The sand flea moved slowly across the child's hand until it fell to the sand right as the tide came in and got them all wet. They heard simultaneous shouts. One from the journalist's wife, telling them to come swimming. The other shout was Bruno's, angry because someone had stolen their towels. A scandal was building. The lifeguard asked him to calm down, while the boy emphatically demanded compensation from the municipality.

Alicia knew she had to go back. She stood up. Incredibly, at that moment, the journalist put his hand on her ankle and whispered her name: Alicia. She turned around, surprised, managing only to respond: I'm sorry, I just wanted to tell you that I wish I'd been your daughter.

Carlos Labbé, one of *Granta's* "Best Young Spanish-Language Novelists," was born in Chile and is the author of six novels—including *Navidad & Matanza* and *Locuela*—and a collection of short stories. In addition to his writings, he is a musician and has released three albums. He is a co-editor at Sangria, a publishing house based in Santiago and Brooklyn, where he translates and runs workshops. He also writes literary essays, the most notable ones on Juan Carlos Onetti, Diamela Eltit, and Roberto Bolaño—three writers whose influence can be seen in *Navidad & Matanza*.

Will Vanderhyden is a translator of Spanish and Latin American fiction. He recently graduated from the MALTS (Masters of Arts in Literary Translation) program at the University of Rochester. In addition to Carlos Labbé, he has translated fiction by Edgardo Cozarinsky, Alfredo Bryce Echenique, Juan Marsé, Rafael Sánchez Ferlosio, and Elvio Gandolfo.

Open Letter—the University of Rochester's nonprofit, literary translation press—is one of only a handful of publishing houses dedicated to increasing access to world literature for English readers. Publishing ten titles in translation each year, Open Letter searches for works that are extraordinary and influential, works that we hope will become the classics of tomorrow.

Making world literature available in English is crucial to opening our cultural borders, and its availability plays a vital role in maintaining a healthy and vibrant book culture. Open Letter strives to cultivate an audience for these works by helping readers discover imaginative, stunning works of fiction and poetry, and by creating a constellation of international writing that is engaging, stimulating, and enduring.

Current and forthcoming titles from Open Letter include works from Argentina, Bulgaria, France, Greece, Iceland, Latvia, Poland, South Africa, and many other countries.

www.openletterbooks.org